THE BOGUS BONDSMAN

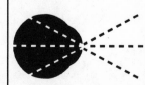

This Large Print Book carries the
Seal of Approval of N.A.V.H.

A GREAT WESTERN DETECTIVE LEAGUE CASE

THE BOGUS BONDSMAN

PAUL COLT

WHEELER PUBLISHING
A part of Gale, a Cengage Company

Farmington Hills, Mich • San Francisco • New York • Waterville, Maine
Meriden, Conn • Mason, Ohio • Chicago

LIBRARY OF CONGRESS CIP DATA ON FILE.
CATALOGUING IN PUBLICATION FOR THIS BOOK
IS AVAILABLE FROM THE LIBRARY OF CONGRESS

ISBN-13: 978-1-4328-4621-3 (softcover)
ISBN-10: 1-4328-4621-3 (softcover)

Published in 2018 by arrangement with Paul Colt

Printed in the United States of America
1 2 3 4 5 6 7 22 21 20 19 18

THE BOGUS BONDSMAN

Prologue

New York
1878

Jay Gould had a habit of winning. He maintained it by making his own rules. Which is another way of saying rules didn't apply to the diminutive financier. His style made enemies and detractors, mostly the victims of his ruthless schemes. He was a shadow to the law. A man removed from his deeds by cutouts, shell corporations, and a heavy veil of deniability. They hated him for it. One fellow speculator thought him wholly loathsome without redeeming humanity. Another characterized him as a "Ruthless predator, satanic in his manipulations." Gould found their venom flattering. He bested them and they hated him for it. He thought it mildly amusing, but only mildly. The only thing that truly amused Gould was money, lots of money.

He sat at a neatly clean desk haloed in

lamplight. He studied the security on his blotter, a ten thousand dollar Texas & Pacific Railroad bearer bond, maturing in 1878. One interest coupon remained attached, the others having been previously claimed. He'd purchased it and used it along with other instruments to secure a credit facility for purchase of the railroad's deeply discounted stock. Using the railroad's own debt to finance his takeover amused him. The gains had been handsome, but now it was time to cash out in favor of a more lucrative opportunity. His appetite had turned to the Missouri Pacific. Executing that plan would require cash, more than he could muster at the moment.

The bond gave him pause to reflect. The Texas & Pacific had served its useful purpose. He'd taken his profits on their stock. Their debt might yet provide the additional cash he needed to complete control of the Missouri Pacific. A single ten-thousand-dollar bond wouldn't do. A ladder composed of larger denominations could. He held the blueprint in his hand. He knew of a reliable engraver whose skill might be up to the task. The Don could handle distribution. Gould resigned himself to the prospect. The old lecher would exact his exorbitant percentage. He always did. Of course the crime lord took risks he would never accept for himself. He would simply add a couple of bonds to the ladder to cover his cost.

Chicago
The dark-eyed stranger's sodden shoes squeezed moisture on rain-slicked cobbles as he rounded the corner to a backstreet block of shabby storefronts. He turned his collar up against a sharp wind gust. He found the shop he sought in the middle of the block. He'd had some unusual assignments from his anonymous client over the years, but this one might take the prize. Prizes didn't matter. The client paid him handsomely for his services. A disbarred lawyer, the Counselor, as his employer knew him, understood the role he played representing his client. He was an anonymous agent, a well-paid break in any chain of evidence that might link his client to the crimes or the less than ethical dealings he was paid to facilitate. Given his experience in such matters, he had proven himself able to evade detection, thereby providing his client and himself a further layer of protection.

He reached the soot-stained storefront in the middle of the block. A window sign painted in chipped gold letters proclaimed K. Gottschaft, Master Engraver. He glanced behind him. No one moved on the street. He opened the door to the jangle of a visitor bell. Inside gray light filtered through the grime-streaked front window. The place smelled of printers' ink and harsh solvents. He paused, allowing his eyes to adjust to the dim light. A scarred wooden counter separated the entry from a dark-shadowed work area cluttered by a lamplit desk, ink-stained flatbed printing press, racks of storage cabinetry, and a long workbench at the back of the room. How did anyone work in such dingy surroundings? Of course the answer wouldn't matter for long.

A bent figure shuffled out of the shadows. A pinched little man with an oily pate thatched in thin wisps of white hair. Wire-rimmed spectacles rode the bridge of a birdlike beak. Thin lips pressed a tight line over even rows of tobacco-stained yellow teeth.

"May I help you?"

"Are you Herr Gottschaft?"

He nodded. "Kurt Gottschaft at your service."

"I'm told you may be able to help me."

He cocked his head. "Help vith vhat?"

The Counselor laid a worn leather case on the counter and withdrew a single engraved sheet. He slid it across the counter.

The engraver ran a gnarled finger with a cracked nail over the finish. He picked up the sheet and turned, allowing the pale window light to illuminate the engraving. He lifted his spectacles to his forehead and fitted a jeweler's loop to one eye. He moved the sheet left, then right. He tilted the sheet to a flat angle. In a practiced motion he allowed the loop to drop from his eye and replaced his spectacles. He laid the sheet on the counter.

"A fine piece of vork, vhat is it you require, Herr . . . ?"

"My name is unimportant. I need twelve of these. Can you reproduce the plate and print them?"

He lifted his bushy white brows above smudged spectacles. "You mean can I produce twelve counterfeit bonds?"

"They aren't counterfeit unless they are negotiated."

"A fine point of law."

"To you it is engraving and printing. Can you do it?"

"The engraving and printing? Of course. The risk is another matter. Twelve of these might fetch one hundred twenty thousand dollars. This is a good deal of money."

The stranger shook his head and tapped

the engraved amount. "You must add a zero."

The engraver's eyes bulged. He glanced again at the certificate.

"Can you do it?"

"Dis is expensive vork."

"Five thousand, half now, the balance when I pick up the plate and the certificates."

The engraver's eyes bulged again.

"How long will it take?"

"A month, perhaps six weeks."

"You have five."

CHAPTER ONE

Shady Grove
Denver
May, 1908

My name is Robert Brentwood. I am employed as a reporter for the *Denver Tribune,* though, in this venture, I've come to compile a story of the Great Western Detective League for a second book I expect to pen. I stumbled on reports of this association of law enforcement officers and professionals in the archives of the *Denver Tribune* something over a year ago. Imagine my surprise when I discovered the following fall that the mastermind behind this storied network of crime fighters was alive and comfortably ensconced at the Shady Grove Rest Home and Convalescent Center. My nascent writing career seemed foreordained by the discovery. I introduced myself to the principal, one Colonel David J. Crook, and prevailed upon the irascible old gentleman to indulge me with his stories. Having little better to do, he agreed. That set in motion nothing less than the complete transformation of my life, which, as you shall see, continues with this writing.

The colonel began his tale with the pursuit and demise of the notorious outlaw train robber Sam Bass. The archived case that more recently caught my eye was one of a rather different nature. The news accounts were sufficiently vague so as to elicit more questions than answers. Curious, I meant for the colonel to supply those answers.

I arrived at Shady Grove that Saturday morning as had become my custom since embarking on these endeavors the previous year. The reception nurse smiled as I entered the solarium.

"The colonel is waiting on the veranda. Shall I tell her you're here?"

The twinkle in her eye was meant to confound me. The *her* she referred to is the person of Miss Penny O'Malley, the nurse charged with the colonel's care and the woman I'd been seeing since shortly after my introduction to this enterprise.

"That won't be necessary." I returned her smile. "I know where to find the colonel."

She nodded ever so slightly, acknowledging the futility of my attempt at deception.

Women, one moment they insist on the pretense of propriety and in the next fritter it away in girlish gabble.

Colonel Crook sat in his wheelchair with a ramrod straight air that denied the ravages of his advancing years. He preferred the sharp mountain air of early spring on the broad veranda to the stuffy, overly warm interior maintained for the residents. The only concession he permitted to the cold, a blanket wrapped about his legs. He had thick white hair, bushy muttonchops, and alert blue eyes that managed to retain the calm, cool measure of his younger years. He still possessed the keen, intuitive wit that distinguished his career as a master investigator and driving force behind the legendary Great Western Detective League. The daring deeds of that distinguished organization and the countless adventures recorded in their case files were etched like a map in the wrinkled features of the man who recalled them.

"Good afternoon, Robert."

He never turned in his chair. "Good day to you, Colonel. How did you know it was me?"

"Your footfall was expected."

"That transparent am I?"

"Most people are. And by that bulge in

your jacket, I see our bargain remains intact."

I made a careful circumspection of our surroundings to ensure no one was present to observe our weekly exchange of contraband. I handed him a bottle of whiskey in exchange for his empty one. Both were promptly concealed, the colonel's in his lap robe, mine in a jacket pocket.

"So what's on your mind now that we've properly dealt with Sam Bass?"

"I have come across another case that intrigues me, though I must say the reports are sketchy and scant in detail."

"That would be the case of the Bogus Bondsman, I'm sure."

I sat back stunned. "Why, yes. How did you know?"

"There's a reason those reports are spare of detail."

"What's that?"

He smiled. "All in good time, my impatient young friend. All in good time."

"All right then, where do we begin?"

Crook let his gaze drift up the mountain. "The perpetration in this case was rather elaborate and well under way by the time we became involved. You may recall Briscoe Cane prevailed upon Beau Longstreet to leave the employ of the Pinkerton Agency and sign on with our Great Western Detective League."

"I do recall that. Did Longstreet take Cane up on the offer?"

"He did. He took some time out to dally along the way as Longstreet was wont to do, but he did finally join us."

"That widow?"

"That widow."

Silver Slipper
Denver
1878

Silver Slipper my ass. Longstreet surveyed the saloon from the batwings. Why in hell would a man like Cane favor a dump like this? If the Great Western Detective League were as lucrative as he made out, he could surely afford a watering hole with something more by way of amenities. Beauregard *Beau* Longstreet stood tall, muscular, and handsome. His family roots ran deep in the old South. He came from the fringes of the more prominent Longstreet line best known for his famous cousin, who served on Robert E. Lee's general staff. Beau had never been West Point material. He parlayed his family name into a junior officer's appointment and rose to the rank of captain before the war ended. Humiliated in defeat, he

17

drifted west, reaching St. Louis penniless. He signed on as a Pinkerton guard out of necessity. He soon demonstrated a knack for protection. They'd done a good deal of defending in the later stages of the war. His experience as a field commander distinguished his performance. He gained greater responsibility in his assignments as the company followed the railroads and goldfields west.

A devil-may-care ladies' man by nature, on a case he was a circumspect investigator, logical and intuitive. He had a knack for the subtle clue, the overlooked fact, a cold trail, and human nature.

He spotted Briscoe Cane at a corner table with his back to the wall. The man had changed little since Round Rock. His lean weather-lined features might have been stitched out of old saddle leather. He had a hawk-sharp nose and cold gray eyes animated by some inner light. The only change Longstreet noticed was that his formerly shoulder-length hair, gray before its time, was better barbered. Undoubtedly a concession to his newfound prosperity. His angular, hickory-hard frame still had that deceptively awkward appearance. For the object of one of his pursuits, misestimating his appearance might prove fatal. Cane possessed cat-quick reflexes and deadly accuracy in the use of a veritable arsenal of weaponry concealed under a black frock coat.

He favored a pair of fine balanced bone blades, one sheathed behind the .44 holster rig on his right hip and the other in his left boot. He could draw and throw with either hand fast enough to defeat most men at their gun draw. He was equally fast with the Colt and a .41 caliber Forehand & Wadsworth Bull Dog rigged for cross draw at his back. Some might consider a spur-rigger pocket pistol a less than manly weapon. Such a notion would sadly misestimate Cane's use of it. Those that harbored such foolish notions seldom did so for long. On the trail he carried a Henry rifle that could pluck out a man's eye at a thousand paces. When called for, he possessed a master craftsman's skill with explosives. Were it not for the staunch religious foundation afforded by his upbringing, he might have enjoyed a more lucrative career as an assassin than the pursuit he had as a bounty hunter.

Longstreet pushed through the batwings and crossed the stained plank floor through a smoky haze. Cane lifted one eye beneath a thick bush of brow. He pushed a chair from under the table with an unseen boot.

"Longstreet. About time you got here. She must have been one hell of a good time."

"Nice to see you too, Briscoe. I'm not one to kiss and tell, but I wasn't in any particular hurry to leave Buffalo Station."

"But you did."

"I did when the time came."

"So are you still wasting your time workin' for Pinkerton or are you here to join the league?"

"If the offer's still open, I'd be pleased to meet your Colonel Crook."

"It's a bit late for that today. I'll introduce you to him in the morning. In the meantime sit down and let's have a drink."

Longstreet looked around. "You really hang around here?"

He crooked a half smile. "You don't approve? Not up to your Pinkerton standards?"

"You could do better."

"Sure I could. What's the point? People leave me alone here. Things get less complicated that way." He waved the bartender over with a glass and poured.

Chicago

A single lamp spread an oily yellow sheen over the work table, creating an island of light in the darkened workshop. The engraver bent over his work shrouded in shadow. He worked with the aid of a jeweler's loop fitted to his eye and an awl honed to a needle-fine point. He consulted the bond affixed to the workbench beside the emerging copy. He labored methodically, etching the image in a special wax-like coating to expose the bare copper plate beneath. Line by line, point by point, dash by dash, he drew with painstaking attention to detail.

He stretched. The bunched knots in his back and neck burned. He glanced at the calendar on his desk. So much work, so little time. He bent to his etching again. He began in the top right corner inspecting his work, comparing it to the image of the authentic bond he carried in his mind's eye. *Das ist gut.* He drew a pocket watch from a vest pocket, flipped the cover open in a practiced motion, and noted the time. Ten thirty-three. He yawned and shook his head, another long day.

He felt his way through the gloom to the stove and poured the bitter dregs from his coffee pot. He took a swallow. Two weeks into the assignment and the plate was less than half complete. It must be finished in two weeks time to allow for washing, printing, and drying. He drained his cup. Another hour or two he resolved. It did no good to work to exhaustion. A man could not retain his concentration. He might become careless. The coffee must give him another hour or two. The work could not be finished any other way.

CHAPTER TWO

Great Western Detective League
Denver, 1878

Cane arrived at my office the next morning accompanied by a handsome brute of a fellow I didn't know, though deduction preceded his introduction.

"Colonel, may I present Beau Longstreet. You may recall I mentioned him following the Sam Bass case."

"Why, yes, I do. Pinkerton, wasn't he? My pleasure, Mr. Longstreet."

"Please, call me Beau."

Firm grip. "How may I be of assistance?"

"Briscoe has been telling me about your Great Western Detective League. He tells me I'd be more profitably employed in your service than that of my current employer. I've come to see for myself."

"Splendid. Please have a seat. Briscoe?"

"Thanks all the same, Colonel. I've heard the story. I've some things to take care of so

I'll leave you two to discuss Beau's future. Beau, I'll meet you at the Palace for lunch."

"See you then."

Cane took his leave.

"Now then, Beau, Cane tells me you are a competent investigator. Perhaps you would tell me something of yourself. Do I suppose from your name and accent you fought for the other side in the war?"

"True, though my cousin received most of the notoriety for that. I hope you'll not hold that against me on top of my Pinkerton station."

"Nonsense, the war is over. How did you come to join Pinkerton?"

"My family lost the plantation following the war. I drifted west. Took a guard job with Pinkerton in St. Louis to make ends meet. One thing led to another. I worked my way up from there."

"I see. How much has Cane told you about the Great Western Detective League?"

"Enough to know he's pleased with his arrangement. I've seen the league at work in the Bass case. Briscoe profited handsomely by his involvement with you. I drew my salary from Pinkerton along with my next assignment."

"What was that?"

"Minor case of railroad agent fraud."

"We don't handle many cases like that. We prefer to spend our time on higher profile cases. The pursuits are more lucrative."

"How does that work?"

"The Great Western Detective League is an association of law enforcement professionals across the west. We take on cases where substantial rewards or retainers are offered. Most often we are retained by those who have suffered a loss to recover their property. We offer an advantage over local law enforcement whose jurisdictions are limited. We, on the other hand, are able to cross jurisdictions."

"Pinkerton crosses jurisdiction. That's the reason businesses like railroads that cross jurisdictions hire us to protect their interests."

"I understand. We, on the other hand, are able to facilitate cooperation with local law enforcement in almost any jurisdiction."

"I saw that down in Texas."

"How much cooperation does Pinkerton enjoy?"

"Very little."

"Precisely. We are able to gain cooperation because law enforcement officials are eligible to become members of the Great Western Detective League and participate in the rewards of our work. As a field operative, you would receive sixty percent of the proceeds from your cases."

"What happens to the rest?"

"I take twenty-five percent to fund operation of the league. Fifteen percent is reserved and used to pay an annual bonus in equal shares to all league members. Those bonuses can add up to a tidy sum over the course of a year. They ensure that we keep everyone interested in cooperating. Cooperation consists of providing information and assistance in a local jurisdiction. We get superior results because we give and receive the best information. Superior results assure us the most lucrative opportunities."

"Impressive, Colonel, it truly is impressive. It's simple and I've seen it work. Have you a place in your organization for a man like me?"

"According to Cane, I must. Will you join us?"

"I will."

"Excellent. When will you notify our friend, Lord Kingsley?"

"Lord Kingsley?"

"Not really landed gentry. We sometimes call him that for all his English starch."

"I see. Well, I've got time before I meet Cane for lunch."

"Good. Then we shall expect you to start

as soon as you put your affairs in order. Where would you like to take up your place?"

"Where?"

"Our operatives span the west. You can live anywhere you like."

Longstreet glanced around. "It looks like Denver is where the action is."

"A wise observation, my boy."

"I shall need to find a place to stay. The Palace is a fine hotel, but it is a little expensive."

"Widow O'Rourke operates a respectable boarding house two blocks from here."

Pinkerton Office

Longstreet found Kingsley in his cluttered office seated at a desk mounded in paper. Reginald Kingsley lacked the look of a Pinkerton operative, much less master detective and managing director of the Denver office. He had the pinched appearance of a librarian or college professor with alert blue eyes, delicate features, and a full mustache tinged in the barest hint of gray. He favored wool jackets in subdued hues of herringbone or tweed. When called for, he topped himself off in a stylish bowler, properly square to his head. He carried a silver-tipped cane he might wield as a baton or break into a rapier-like blade. In the field, he carried a short-barreled .44 Colt pocket pistol cradled in a shoulder holster. He could disappear in a crowd, or turn himself out in a chameleon array of disguises selected to suit his purposes. He dripped comfortable British charm that easily insinuated itself into the trust of the unsuspecting criminal.

"Ah, Longstreet, old boy, welcome to Denver. I thought you might have taken up permanent residence in, what was it again?"

"Buffalo Station."

"Oh, yes. Quite right. She must have been a most disarming attraction to hold onto the likes of you this long. Well, you're here now; that's all that matters. I shall have to check the blotter to see what's up for your next assignment."

"That won't be necessary."

"Oh? What do you mean?"

"I'm leaving the agency."

"Oh, dear, my boy, whatever for?"

"I've accepted another position."

"What sort of position, may I ask?"

"With the Great Western Detective League."

"Good heavens, you'd leave the employ of 'The Eye That Never Sleeps,' the most prestigious private detective agency in the

28

world, for that loose confederation?"

"Yes."

"But you're a Pinkerton. That means something. It's steady, secure work."

"The league pays better."

"I see. Well, of course, I'm not at liberty to promise anything, but perhaps we could review the matter of your remuneration."

"My what?"

"Your salary."

"That won't be necessary, Mr. Kingsley. I've already accepted the position."

"I'm sorry to hear that, Beau. Very well then, I'm sure we shall see one another in the field. I wish you the best of luck. You'll need it."

Shady Grove

I was so engrossed in the colonel's tale I must confess I failed to notice her approach.

"Time for lunch, Colonel."

Penny O'Malley was the colonel's nurse. I'd admired her from the beginning of my association with Colonel Crook. I saw her for the first time as a vision in a pale blue dress with a clean white apron. The soft form of a woman's figure could not be denied by the severity of an institutional uniform. She had a kind face, pert lips, and short, curled dark hair crowned by a nurse's cap. Her eyes were as soft as melted chocolates filled with caramel. She composed her pretty lips in the hint of a smile reminiscent of Mona Lisa. She had a velvety voice with a smidgen of Irish brogue. A sprinkle of angel-kiss freckles graced the bridge of her turned-up nose. A light scent of vanilla ice cream flavored her presence. I'd been smitten from the first, speechless and tongue-tied until the colonel inserted himself to introduce us. We'd been seeing each other ever since, providing endless opportunities to indulge the old gentleman's penchant for teasing. I recovered with a smile she returned.

"You hear that, Robert? She calls it lunch. Thin soup to soften day-old bread served with a cup of dishwater they call coffee. The only appeal is that most often it induces a satisfying afternoon nap."

"A silver lining for every cloud," Penny said.

She could put a sweet point on anything where I was concerned.

"I expect you two have plans for this evening."

"You'd rather not know."

"Not know? Robert, you must understand I live vicariously through your romantic exploits. Whatever else is there to give me pleasure?"

I lifted an eyebrow to the bulge in his lap robe where he'd concealed his bottle of contraband whiskey, the gesture alone sufficient to silence the old curmudgeon's incessant teasing.

"All right then, don't tell me. Leave it to my imagination. The rumors only become juicier for the speculation."

She threw up her hands. "We plan to see a motion picture show if you must know."

He smiled. "And top it off with a hot fudge sundae, I'll wager."

"I hadn't thought about that, Colonel, but it seems a capital idea. What do you say, Penny?"

She smiled her Mona Lisa and turned his chair.

"Until next week then, Robert; and remember, you owe all of this to me."

CHAPTER THREE

Chicago

Predawn gray light seeped into the workshop through streaked window grime. The smell of freshly brewed coffee bubbling on the stove mingled with the scents of paper, ink, and strong chemicals. The engraver lit the workbench lamp. He fixed the jeweler's loop to his eye and bent over the last of his work from the previous evening. He studied the pattern etched to the plate. *Jah, dis vill do nicely.*

He stood, dropped the loop from his eye, and shuffled to the stove. He poured a cup of coffee and blew into the fragrant steam. He had one more week to complete his commission. This day would determine the result of four weeks of painstaking work. Today he would bite the plate.

He crossed the workshop to a bench, took a sip of coffee, and set the cup beside the acid bath. This part of the process was beyond his skilled hands. The acid would do its work on the exposed copper, etching his engraving into the surface of the metal. If he'd done his work skillfully, the acid would expose it. Once the biting was complete, he had only to wash away the wax coating and prepare to make the printing impressions.

The stock rested, neatly stacked beside the printing press. A pot of the precise shade of ink sat safely on the opposite side of the press. Twelve impressions, one million two hundred thousand dollars in perfectly counterfeit bearer bonds. He rubbed his chin, somehow five thousand dollars seemed a paltry commission for such extravagant work. He'd created a masterpiece. The client would take the plate. Indeed the plate could produce many more impressions than twelve. The value of his crowning achievement might prove priceless at a compensation of five thousand dollars to the master.

Palace Hotel
Denver
Longstreet left Kingsley and walked the few short blocks to his hotel. He found Cane, looking out of place in the opulent Victorian elegance of the hotel lobby.

"How'd it go?"

"Just fine. We're now on the same team."

"I thought as much. When will you tell Kingsley?"

"Already have."

"How'd he take it?"

"About what you'd expect. Couldn't believe it at first. Closed the book on me once he figured out I was serious. Come on, I'll buy you a beer and a bite to eat in the saloon."

They crossed the lobby to the deserted saloon and took a corner table. A portly bartender in a clean, crisp apron approached the table.

"What'll it be, gents?"

"What's for lunch?" Longstreet said.

"Roast beef and mashed."

"Okay with you, Cane?"

He nodded.

"Make it two of those and two beers."

The waiter set off to fill their order.

"So where do you figure to hang your hat?"

"Here's as good as anyplace."

"Hmm, I kind of thought you might go back to Buffalo Station. Seemed like you took quite a shine to the place." His eye twinkled at the unspoken reference to an attractive hotel owner.

"We ran our course. Might go back some

time for a visit, but neither one of us wanted any more than what we had. Denver's as good a place as any."

"What are you going to do about a place to live?"

"Colonel Crook recommended Mrs. O'Rourke's boarding house."

"Nice place, a little too civilized for my taste."

The waiter arrived with two frosty mugs.

"I got a room upstairs at the Silver Slipper."

Longstreet shook his head. "I'd think those were all cribs for the doves."

"Probably were when business was better."

"Why stay there?"

"Like I said, they leave me alone. I get my meals, drinks, and don't have far to go to bed."

"I don't get it, a man with your religious principles. I should think you'd be more comfortable in a parsonage somewhere."

"Folks at a parsonage ain't much in need of righteous thinking. Sinners, now those folks can use a righteous word now and then."

The waiter arrived with lunch.

"Never figured you for a preacher."

"I ain't. Just God-fearin' when I need to be."

Longstreet had little difficulty finding the boarding house Colonel Crook directed him to. A stately three-story whitewashed clapboard structure situated in the center of a tree-lined block. It sat behind a wrought-iron fence, fronted by carefully tended gardens. He swung through the gate and climbed the steps to a broad front porch. Frosted cut-glass windows with lace curtains bordered the polished front door. He tapped the brass knocker. Moments later light footfalls tatted the wood floor beyond.

The door opened to something of a surprise. The colonel's reference to "Widow O'Rourke's" boarding house conjured up a rather different expectation to the vision that greeted him at the door.

"Yes?"

"I, ah, I'm told I might find a Mrs. O'Rourke here."

"You've found her. I'm Madeline O'Rourke. And you, sir?"

"Beau, Beauregard Longstreet. Colonel Crook suggested I might find rooming accommodations here."

She eyed him up and down.

He returned the favor. Madeline

O'Rourke presented a fine figure of a woman, with wholesome good looks, waves of velvet auburn hair, and a flawless complexion splashed lightly across the bridge of an upturned nose with girlish golden freckles.

"Won't you come in, Mr. Longstreet?"

She spoke the buttery brogue of her immigrant heritage. Longstreet imagined he noticed a mischievous twinkle at the back of her dark-green eyes. She stepped aside to let him in. The entry foyer floor and the hallway beyond shone off the smell of fresh wax. A scent of freshly baked bread hung in the air.

"Come this way." She led him into a comfortably appointed parlor and showed him to the settee. "Please have a seat." She took the facing wing chair.

"Have you a room for me, ma'am?"

She knit her brow. "We shall see. I must tell you I am particular about my tenants. I have a reputation to protect and I'm not yet persuaded you would be good for that."

"Was it something I said?"

"Not yet, it's just a feeling I have. Now tell me something of yourself, Mr. Longstreet. You're from the south, I take it. Where are you from? What brings you to Denver?"

"My family roots are in South Carolina. I came west after the war. For the past few years I've been employed by the Pinkerton Detective Agency. I've only this morning decided to accept a position with Colonel Crook's Great Western Detective League."

"So you are a man of the law, then."

"Yes, ma'am."

She winced.

"What sort of work will you do for Colonel Crook?"

"I expect to take field assignments."

"So you'll travel then."

"Yes." *No ma'am, no wince.*

"Your residence here would be a place to hang your hat between assignments."

He nodded.

"I suppose that might work, provided of course you agree to abide by the rules."

"Rules?"

"My house rules. Breakfast is served at seven, dinner at six thirty. No female guests beyond the parlor. No gambling or late night carousing on the premises. Strong drink is permitted only in moderation and I am the sole judge of moderation."

"There's a mercy."

"I beg your pardon?"

"An Irish lass in charge of moderation where liquor is imbibed."

38

She flushed, caught a merry chuckle in her throat, and fixed him with a cool green reprimand. "I am indeed that judge. And to be perfectly clear on the point, I have a strict policy against fraternizing with my tenants. Is that understood?"

"Yes, ma'am."

She scowled. "If you'll come this way, I'll show you the room I have available." She led the way to a broad staircase climbing out of the foyer. "It's on the third floor, I'm afraid. I hope that's not too inconvenient."

"No, ma'am." She plainly didn't appreciate him calling her that. He smiled. It might break the ice. He followed her hips up the stairs. *No fraternization* indeed; rules were made to be broken.

The room was large and airy with windows on two sides. The furnishings were comfortably simple with a small writing desk, a wing chair, armoire, washbasin, and bed.

"The rent is twenty dollars a month with one month on deposit in advance. Is that acceptable?"

"Yes, ma'am."

"Oh please, Mr. Longstreet, if you are going to live here I simply can't abide you calling me that. It feels like a dried-up old husk. My friends call me Maddie."

"Very well then, Maddie, you must call me Beau." He topped it off with a charming southern smile.

Her cheeks warmed. "Very well then, Beau."

I have a strict policy . . . I do.

CHAPTER FOUR

Chicago

Printing required skill and care. In more prosperous times the engraver hired skilled craftsmen to do the work. These days, times being what they were, he did it himself. He had two days left to fill the order, one to finish the printing and one to complete the drying. He'd worked through the morning and early afternoon to complete the last of the printing impressions. He counted eleven printed sheets hanging on the drying line, one million one hundred thousand dollars in railroad bearer bonds, every bit as valuable as cash.

He wiped ink onto the surface of the plate, pressing it into the incising with a soft cloth. He carefully wiped the residue clean. The twelfth sheet of paper soaked in a tray. He drew it out, shook off the excess moisture, and patted it damp. The fibers were dampened so they could be pressed into the etched grooves, thus acquiring the print. He set the plate on the bed of the rolling press and aligned the paper to the plate. He covered it with a heavy blanket that would distribute pressure evenly across the surface of the plate. He rolled the press, removed the blanket, and beheld the twelfth bond. Gently the engraver removed it from the plate and clipped it to the drying line. The order was complete, save the drying. He had only to wash the plate for delivery to the client with his order.

He bent to remove the plate from the press and set it on the workbench for washing. He paused. The idea had nibbled at the back of his consciousness for weeks. He was one printing impression away from retiring to a modest villa in Bavaria. Just one printing impression away, who would know? Who would complain? The criminal who hired him? Not likely. In fact, when the fraud came to light, as it must, the criminal would be blamed. *Kurt Gottschaft vould haf long ago left the country.* He set a fresh sheet of paper to soak.

Two Days Later

The visitor bell clanged near closing. The engraver expected it. The Counselor closed the door. Shoe leather and floorboard creaks followed him across the shop to the counter. The old man shuffled out of the workshop carrying a small bundle wrapped in brown paper.

"Guten abend."

"Have you finished?"

He nodded, passing the bundle across the counter.

The visitor drew a pearl-handled pocket knife and slit the twine that was binding the bundle. He unfolded the wrapping. The package contained a folder and the plate wrapped in clean cloth. He drew a bond out of the folder and held it up to the feeble light. Satisfied, he replaced it and counted the others. He unwrapped the plate and examined the etching. He refolded the plate in its cloth wrapping and placed it inside a battered leather case along with the folder.

"Is everything in satisfactory order?"

"A fine piece of work, Herr Gottschaft. You are to be congratulated."

The engraver smiled and nodded.

The Counselor reached into his coat as if for a wallet. He drew out a .41 Colt pocket pistol and leveled it at the old man, wide-eyed behind his spectacles. The muzzle flash exploded with a roar that fell on deaf ears. The old man pitched back, a dark stain spreading across his breast.

The Counselor gathered his battered case and crossed the workshop to a back door that opened onto an alley. He looked into dark silence left and right, then disappeared into the night.

Denver

Longstreet presented himself for dinner at precisely 6:30. He'd dressed in coat and forehand, intent on a good first impression. He was greeted by the appraising eye of a stout woman in a severe dark-blue dress whose white hair piled high on her head.

"You must be the new border. Abigail Fitzwalter." She extended a firm sturdy hand.

"Beau Longstreet, Mrs. Fitzwalter, pleased to make your acquaintance."

"Longstreet, now there's a rather infamous ring to northern ears."

"My cousin, ma'am. I hope you'll not hold that against me."

"Heavens no, the war is over and good riddance to it too. Have you recently arrived in Denver?"

"I have. I've accepted a position with the Great Western Detective League."

"I must say, I'm not familiar with that. Are you a law officer then?"

"In a manner of speaking, the league acts

as a private detective agency."

"I see. That must be very exciting."

"It can be at times."

"Ah, there you are, Mr. Longstreet. Punctual, I like that." Maddie stood at the door to the kitchen with a steaming platter of roast beef and stewed vegetables.

"I aim to please, ma'am."

She set the platter on the table. "Ma'am? I thought we had an understanding?"

"That would make me Beau, ma'am."

"Yes, Beau, I, ah, forgot."

"You wound me, my dear. I've only just arrived and already I'm forgotten."

"Wounded is it? I can't imagine a man of your self-estimation would have much experience with such a thing. And I am not your dear. You do remember the rules I trust."

"Now there's the spirit I'd expect, Maddie girl."

Mrs. Fitzwalter raised a curious brow.

"Maddie will do. I see you've met Mrs. Fitzwalter. Take a seat. T'will be only the three of us this evening. Mr. Brighton is away on business." She took her seat at the head of the table.

The walled hacienda sat on a low mesa surrounded by a broad plain. The Counselor had visited it and its mysterious Patron on two previous occasions. It had taken the personal recommendation of his client to arrange the meetings. Don Victor Carnicero, it seemed, was nearly as obsessed with his obscurity as the Counselor's client. The Patron, as he was known to his shadowy network of operatives, provided a variety of services beyond the scale the Counselor could manage.

As instructed, he'd rented a carriage and driven to the hacienda from Santa Fe, arriving as the last rays of setting sun turned the distant mountain peaks orange and purple. Two of the Don's men met him at the gate. He surrendered his weapon before being searched and was admitted to the compound. He was shown to a guest room where he could freshen up before meeting the Don for drinks and dinner.

An hour later, the Don's man, a muscular mountain with an ugly scar who served as his bodyguard, showed him into a large formal library warmed in the glow of candlelight. The literary collection was truly impressive, though considering the Patron's

46

line of work, the Counselor wondered, as he had on a previous visit, how much the collection might owe to a passion for literature or the pretense of legitimate pursuit. An interesting question to which the Counselor reconciled he'd never know the answer.

Bootheels clicked the tile passage, approaching the library.

The Patron, Don Victor Carnicero, carried himself with a patrician bearing and an aura of power that suggested a larger stature than his average height. Handsome still in the echo of youthful vigor, waves of white hair and a neatly trimmed mustache set off a swarthy complexion with the patina of polished leather. He filled the room with the presence of a benevolent grandfather were it not for his eyes. Deep-set and black, they glittered with an inner fire that smoldered in equanimity or enflamed in rage. Little ruffled his outward demeanor. Only his eyes gave light to a ruthless hard edge.

Patron presided over a shadowy network known to the very few as El Anillo (The Ring). His organization discreetly served the indelicate needs of the rich and powerful. His clients included crooked politicians, organized labor, robber-baron industrialists, affluent anarchists, and wealthy criminals. His specialties included murder for hire, protection, and liquidation of illegal merchandise, all performed in a manner designed to strictly assure client anonymity. All his services came at exorbitant fees as befitting the risk and his client's means of payment.

He smiled broadly in greeting, showing even white teeth. "So, Counselor, we meet again."

The man's handshake was firm. It spoke of a bond, a trust that must never be broken.

"I was about to enjoy a tequila. Would you care to join me?"

"Whiskey, if you don't mind."

"Of course. You Americanos, so few of you have acquired the taste. Felipe, por favor." He spoke to the shadows. "Please, sit down." He indicated wing chairs drawn up around a low polished table.

A waiter in a starched white jacket appeared with drinks and a bowl of papitas.

Don Victor lifted his glass. "Salud." He savored a swallow.

"Now, señor, how may I be of service to my friend?"

The Counselor opened his leather case, drew out a stack of bearer bonds, and passed them across the table to Don Victor.

He fanned the stack. Twelve at one hundred thousand each, he nodded.

"This is a great deal of money. Is there something I am to purchase with it?"

"Cash."

"I see. These must not then be as they appear?"

The Counselor nodded. "Don Victor is very perceptive."

"Our usual fee?"

"Twenty percent."

He gave a mirthless smile. "How soon does my friend need the money?"

"How soon can it be done?"

"With denominations this large arrangements must be made, three, maybe four months."

The Counselor nodded.

Shady Grove

Fading light in the solarium told me our session for the day had fairly flown by. I rested my notepad. "This has the makings of a complex case."

The colonel nodded. "It was a complex case. And merely the first of its kind."

"The bad actors went to great lengths to avoid detection."

"They did and that's what made it so devilishly difficult to bring to a successful conclusion."

"How did you manage it then?"

He shook his white mane. "Robert, my boy, for a writer you have little sense of drama. If I tell you the end of the story at the beginning, what's the point of the story?"

I had no answer for that. Fortunately my lovely Penny rescued me.

"Time for supper, Colonel."

"Supper they call it, Robert. Supper indeed, a brown something and a green something I'd wager, but it wouldn't be sporting to take your money like that. The truth of it is, supper is an excuse to put me back in my place so that the two of you may be off to your evening's enjoyment. What will it be tonight?"

"A quiet dinner," I said.

"Yes, and I'm sure the fare will be a good deal more tasty than what I'm about to be treated to."

"You'll not starve," Penny said.

"And that's the sad truth. Sustenance to see me through to yet another day of sustenance. See what you've to look forward to, boy."

"I'm sure you'll find a way to soothe your discomfort," I said playfully eyeing the bulge under his blanket.

He shot me a warning look. "I'm pleased you can be so sure of my comfort."

50

CHAPTER FIVE

Chicago

He's gone. The gaunt young man with thinning sandy hair shook his head. Heinrich Gottschaft made the short journey from Milwaukee to Chicago after receiving word of his father's murder. As Kurt's only surviving heir, it fell to him to wind up his father's affairs. He'd put the small house in Grant Park up for sale. An auction house had taken the furnishings. All that remained was the shop.

As he inspected the dingy premises, he wondered what might be done with it. Another engraver might see it for a business. Then again, even as a master craftsman his father barely eked out a living. He doubted it would fetch much. He'd place an advertisement for the equipment in the *Tribune* and offer the building for sale or rent. He crossed the gloomy ink-stained floor to the workbench, making a mental

51

list of the salable equipment items.

He turned to his father's old wooden desk situated near the service counter. He struck a match and lit the desk lamp. He trimmed the wick. Yellow light illuminated the desktop and pooled on the floor. Brown stain marked the place where his father had fallen. *Why?* Why would anyone shoot a harmless old man in such cold-blooded fashion? It made no sense. He drew back the desk chair and sat against the complaint of the springs. The bottom drawer contained a few unpaid bills. The second drawer, a ledger book with neat rows of numbers recorded in an even hand. The top drawer contained an order pad and pencils. The desk drawer opened to a folder of the sort that might contain a customer's order. Inside he felt a single sheet of a fine linen paper. He drew it out and let his eyes wander over the printed image. It was a bond, a Texas & Pacific Railroad bond in the amount of one hundred thousand dollars. *What on earth was his father doing with an instrument of such value?* He couldn't possibly have purchased it. His father's jeweler's loop lay beside the folder. He fitted it to his eye and studied the image. As a boy he'd worked in the shop. It had given him a rudimentary understanding of engraving. The magnified image enlarged his thinking. His father couldn't have purchased an instrument of such value. *He could have printed it. But why only one?* No, there must have been more. An order printed for a customer, a customer who couldn't risk leaving an engraver who knew them for counterfeits. That was the reason to kill a harmless old man. The question now, what to do?

Cheyenne
Wyoming Territory

Escobar took a room at the U.P. Hotel. It adjoined the Union Pacific Station. The rail line would be essential to Don Victor's plan. Escobar would carry out the Patron's instructions with meticulous care as he always did. Nothing would stop him. A slender man with a wiry build, he moved with the stealth of a scorpion. His features were lean and hard, pockmarked by childhood disease. His left cheek bore the scar of a knife fight that ended the worse for the Indio who cut him. Little was known of his shadowy existence beyond his intense loyalty to the Don. Some speculated privately he might be the Patron's illegitimate son, though any resemblance ended with a violent temper. Ruthless in the extreme, he could be brutally sadistic as he carried out orders without question. Within the Don's inner circle he was known as El Ejecutor, the enforcer.

He paced the small suite colored golden in late afternoon sun. Waiting annoyed him. He checked a silver pocket watch. His contact was late. The Don expected more of his minions. He had no experience in the assignment he'd been given. His part was to represent the Don in dealing with this contact. He would collect the proceeds and distribute them to the client, less the Patron's fee. The transactions might seem confusing, but the amounts were staggering. That much he understood.

A knock at the door intruded on his brooding. He crossed to the door prepared to voice his displeasure. He opened the door. He wasn't prepared for this particular contact. The Don hadn't told him she was a beautiful woman. He would soon learn many things the Don might have mentioned.

"Señor Escobar?"

"Sí."

"Cecile Antoine, may I come in?"

He stepped aside holding the door. The woman cloaked herself in understated Victorian prudence. She favored severe dark colors to the extreme of widow's weeds, depending on the persona she might choose for her work. She wore her chestnut hair pulled back in a severe bun in keeping with the look of a librarian, schoolmarm, or church organist. Under this carefully constructed façade lurked lively hazel eyes, a flawless complexion, and stunning figure. When called to do so, she could advance her will on the unsuspecting with sensuous surprise or her own brand of ruthless abandon. He closed the door.

"Please, have a seat."

She arranged her skirt on the offered settee. "Now, tell me about this engagement."

Engagement? He shrugged, opened the leather case he'd been given, and drew out a bond. "You are to cash these." He handed her the bond.

"How many?"

"Twelve."

"That's a good deal of money."

"Sí."

"It will take some time. That increases the risk."

"You will be well paid."

"How much?"

"Twelve thousand."

"For taking all the risk? No thank you." She handed him the bond and rose.

Patron had warned him of this. "How

much do you require?"

She paused. "Twenty-four thousand."

"I am not permitted to offer more than twenty."

She pursed full lips, moistened by a tip of pink tongue. "Done."

"How will you proceed?"

"This requires some thought. I must construct a scene."

"A scene?"

"Think of me as an actress. I play a part. I must determine what part to play."

"How long will this take?"

Impatient. "I should have an opening by tomorrow."

"Opening?"

"We shall need several scenes and characters if we are to avoid detection long enough to complete this engagement."

Scenes, characters, engagements, Patron must know his business, but this is all most confusing.

Chicago
First National Bank of Chicago

Heinrich Gottschaft worked in a brewery. He had little knowledge of banks and bonds and such. Banks were generally formal imposing structures armed to inspire confidence in the depositor with marble, stone, and steel. He had little use for them. He was paid in cash and lived from payday to payday. This bank certainly looked the part. A massive stone façade mounted by a broad stone stairway to a marble expanse where the banking business took place. His eye traveled to a row of brass cages that separated the bankers from their customers. He found an unoccupied cage. A prim buxom woman with gray hair swept up to the top of her head sized him up and down.

"May I help you?"

He drew the bond out of its folder and slid it across the counter. "I vish to cash this."

Her eyes rounded behind wire-rimmed spectacles. "Come to the end of the counter, Mister . . ."

"Gottschaft, Heinrich Gottschaft."

"Thank you. Let me escort you to the cashier."

He smiled to himself. Even a humble brewery worker merited an escort in a bank when he came to cash a one-hundred-thousand-dollar bond. He followed her across the marble expanse to a polished wooden desk occupied by a pinched man in a dark suit seated before the entry to a massive steel vault.

"Mr. Kimball, Mr. Gottschaft would like

to redeem this bond." She handed the bond to the banker.

"Please, Mr. Gottschaft, have a seat. Thank you, Miss Cromwell." He inspected the bond.

"Have you an account with the bank?"

"No, sir. I am settling my father's estate."

"I see. I'm sorry for your loss. The paying agent for this instrument is the Salmon Chase Bank in New York. We will have to present it for redemption with them. That will take a few days. Perhaps we should have something for you this time next week."

"Do I get a receipt or something for it?"

"If you'd like to open an account we could give you provisional credit."

"I expect to receive the cash."

"Are you quite sure? This is, after all, a rather large sum to go about with on your person. I would certainly advise against it."

"I vill take my chances."

"I see. Then we shall have to not only redeem the bond we shall also have to arrange for the cash. We should be able to wrap all that up by a week from Friday. If you'll wait, I'll only be a moment with your receipt."

New York
Charles Colbert III, cashier at Salmon

Chase Bank, examined the bond. Admittedly he hadn't redeemed many Texas & Pacific construction bonds, but he certainly would have remembered one of a one-hundred-thousand-dollar denomination. Something didn't sit right. He wired Texas & Pacific Treasurer, Carter Sewell, to verify the railroad had issued bonds in a one-hundred-thousand-dollar denomination. Sewell responded two hours later. No bonds had been issued in denominations greater than ten thousand dollars. Colbert had his answer. This bond was a forgery, a very good forgery but a forgery nonetheless.

Chicago

Carter Sewell wired the Pinkerton Detective Agency head office in Chicago with instructions to contact the cashier at First National Bank of Chicago and apprehend the individual or individuals responsible for the bogus bond. Heinrich Gottschaft was taken into custody the following Friday. Under questioning he admitted to finding the bond among his murdered father's personal effects. After considering the senior Gottschaft's occupation and the circumstances surrounding his untimely demise, the lead Pinkerton investigator determined it highly likely that the Gottschaft bond was part of a larger plot. He expected additional bonds would likely be presented for payment. He recommended the Texas & Pacific offer a reward for the apprehension of those responsible. Texas & Pacific subsequently offered a ten thousand dollar reward.

CHAPTER SIX

Cheyenne Union Bank

Franklin Pierpont glanced up from the reconciliation statement for the bank's previous day's business. *Stunning* was all he could think. Not the numbers, the woman who'd just entered the lobby. She glanced around the lobby, her eyes coming to rest on his desk beside the vault. She crossed the sun-splashed hardwood, her heels tapping a purposeful tattoo. She smiled, understated warmth in the greeting.

"Might you be the cashier?"

He nodded, returning her smile as he rose from his desk. "Franklin Pierpont at your service, Miss . . ."

"St. James, Cecile St. James." She extended a businesslike hand.

"Please have a seat, Miss St. James. How may Cheyenne Union be of service this morning?"

"I wish to secure a letter of credit."

"Splendid. I'm sure we can accommodate that. In what amount were you thinking?"

She lifted her chin ever so slightly. "One hundred thousand dollars." She said it as casually as observing the weather.

The banker's eyes revealed surprise. The rest of his demeanor said nothing. "That's rather a large sum. May I ask what it is for?"

"I plan to purchase a ranch."

"Wouldn't a mortgage be a more conventional vehicle for such a purchase?"

"I'm not inclined to take on the debt and the seller is in need of a swift closing."

"Then how do you plan to secure the line?"

"With this." She drew a Texas & Pacific bearer bond from her bag and laid it on the desk.

"I see. Well this should certainly cover the facility. I can have the letter drawn up for you by later this afternoon."

"If you don't mind, I'll wait."

Her smile was positively dazzling.

"Of course, I'm at your service."

Cecile returned to the U.P. Hotel just after lunch. She climbed the stairs to the second floor and knocked at Escobar's suite. The ferret-like little man let her in.

"Have you got it?"

She handed him the letter of credit. "Now about my fee, half now and the balance when we finish."

"Make yourself comfortable. I'll return with your fee within the hour."

The Cheyenne Continental Express office traced its roots to the Black Hills gold rush. Gold was a commodity that required transport and transfer services. The venerable money order filled a need for transport services that did not require a freight wagon or strongbox and armed guards. It also suited the purpose of anonymity when needed and thus suited the purposes of Don Victor Carnicero and his anonymous client. Escobar purchased three money orders, two in the amount of ten thousand dollars and one in the amount of eighty thousand dollars. He sent ten thousand to Don Victor in Santa Fe. He posted the eighty thousand dollar order to a Chicago post office address. He used the second ten thousand dollar order to pay Cecile Antoine who boarded the next westbound train for Laramie.

Two days later Continental Express presented the letter of credit for payment at the Cheyenne Union Bank. Satisfied the ranch purchase must have concluded successfully, Franklin Pierpont forwarded the bond for redemption at Salmon Chase. A week later Salmon Chase notified Texas & Pacific and Cheyenne Union that the bond was counterfeit. Texas & Pacific notified the Pinkerton head office in Chicago.

Laramie

The gold leaf window sign proclaimed Laramie Cattleman's Bank. Cecile paused to check her reflection in the window. The lines of her letter of credit story worked perfectly in Cheyenne. She saw no need to change them for Laramie. With the opening act behind her, speed became the most important element to success. Time was her ally only so long as she stayed ahead of the news that the bonds were counterfeit.

She entered the lobby and spotted her mark, a portly banker who looked as though he might have slept in his rumpled suit and sweat-stained linen. Did they all sit at desks just outside the vault? Why not? That's where they kept the money. She smiled her most fetching smile.

An hour later she left the bank with a letter of credit. This might prove easier than she'd first expected. The bonds appeared to be good as gold to these unsuspecting bankers. She glanced at the small watch she wore on a ribbon about her neck, time enough to purchase a ticket and catch the next train west for Rawlins.

Denver

The Western Union messenger arrived at the Pinkerton office as Managing Director Reginald Kingsley was preparing to leave for lunch. He signed for the telegram and tipped the lad, sending him on his way. He tore open the envelope and read the message.

> *Texas & Pacific victim of bond forgery operation.*
> *Most recent occurrence Cheyenne Union Bank.*
> *Meet Agent Maples at U.P. Hotel Cheyenne in three days.*
> — *W. Pinkerton*

Hmm, Kingsley thought, *high profile case when it comes off the desk of the Director of Western Operations.*

Shady Grove

"I received a telegram that same morning from the cashier at Cheyenne Union Bank with the offer of a ten thousand dollar reward for the capture of those responsible for defrauding the bank of one hundred thousand dollars in bond forgery. After ascertaining the paying agent, I wired the cashier at Salmon Chase informing him that the league had been retained by Cheyenne Union and could he please advise any pertinent details. He notified me by return wire that the Cheyenne redemption was the second. The first having occurred in Chicago. Texas & Pacific had also offered a ten-thousand-dollar reward for the apprehension of the counterfeiters. I expected there would be more to come. I dispatched Cane and Longstreet to Cheyenne straight away."

"Time for lunch, Colonel."

I'd been so absorbed in the story I'd not heard her come into the solarium.

"Will you be returning this afternoon after my nap, Robert?"

"Not today I'm afraid."

"A somewhat more pressing engagement on such a bright spring day?"

"As a matter of fact, yes. Penny has the afternoon off."

"I might have known where your priorities are concerned. It's enough to make a man question the seriousness of your commitment to this project."

"You cut me to the quick, sir. Surely you

don't begrudge a man a few moments leisure."

"Time is a fleeting thing, Robert. I'm not getting any younger, you know."

"I think he'll make it to next Saturday," Penny said. She seldom joined in on the colonel's teasing, at least willingly.

"You would take his side. All right, then, I know when I'm overmatched. Until next week, then."

CHAPTER SEVEN

Cheyenne Union Bank

The Denver stage rolled into Cheyenne two days later. Cane and Longstreet climbed down at the station on Sixteenth Street across from the depot. The driver unloaded their bags from the boot and set them on the boardwalk. Longstreet checked his watch.

"Two thirty. If we head on over to the bank, we might still catch them before they close." He snapped the case shut, pocketed the watch, and set off up the street. Cheyenne owed its prominence to Grenville Dodge's decision to route the Union Pacific leg of the Pacific railway north of Denver. Denver lamented the slight while Cheyenne prospered for it with the town sprawling north of the tracks.

Longstreet led the way through a door with a shade half drawn against the afternoon sun. He crossed the polished lobby to

68

the banker seated at a desk beside the vault; he reckoned this was the cashier.

"Mr. Pierpont?"

"Yes." He rose to shake hands.

"Beau Longstreet with the Great Western Detective League. This gentleman is Briscoe Cane. We're here about the loss you reported to Colonel Crook."

"I've been expecting you. Please, have a seat." He indicated chairs drawn up beside his desk. "Now where should we begin?"

Longstreet drew a pencil and notepad from his coat pocket. "Tell us what happened in as much detail as you can recall."

"She came in one morning shortly after we opened."

"She?"

"Yes. Said her name was Cecile St. James. Dignified lady, conservatively dressed, yet stunningly beautiful."

"Anything distinguishing, hair color, eyes?"

"I suppose you'd call her hair chestnut. I don't recall much beyond that. She said she wished to secure a letter of credit for the purchase of a ranch. She offered the bond as security for the credit."

"Didn't that strike you as odd? Wouldn't a mortgage have been a more conventional means to finance such a purchase?"

"I did question it. She said the seller desired a quick sale and that she didn't wish to take on the debt. In hindsight I suppose all that was little more than part of the ruse. I saw a Texas & Pacific bond as solid security for the transaction. I thought it better than a mortgaged property in terms of liquidity and constancy in value. Other than the sizeable amount, it seemed a straightforward transaction."

"So you drew the letter of credit and she left."

He nodded.

"What happened next?"

"Continental Express cashed the letter and presented it for payment."

"They provided cash?"

"Money orders."

"The woman," he checked his notes. "Cecile St. James used your letter of credit to purchase a money order."

"I assume it was her, but it could have been someone else. Continental Express protects the confidentiality of its clients."

"Didn't anyone at Continental Express question the nature of the transaction?"

He shook his head. "The letter of credit was in order. They presented it. We honored it. We didn't realize we had a problem until Salmon Chase Bank, the paying agent in

New York, notified us this past week that the bond is a forgery. Frankly not only is the loss serious, the embarrassment and potential damage to the bank's reputation in this community make the matter even worse."

"Do you have any idea where this Cecile St. James might have gone?"

"The Union Pacific spans the continent. She could be anywhere. How do you begin a search like that?"

"We let her lead us to her," Cane said.

The banker glanced from Longstreet to Cane. "That doesn't make for good jest."

"No jest intended. Two bonds have been presented for redemption so far, one in Chicago and one here. That means they probably have more. The question is, where will the gang strike next? That's where the Great Western Detective League comes in. We cast a wide net. If you'd been notified to be on the lookout for counterfeit Texas & Pacific construction bonds, you'd likely have avoided the loss. You might even have been able to notify law enforcement authorities and capture the suspect. That's what we do."

"Let's hope so," he said, wiping sweat from his pate with a linen kerchief.

"Is there anything else you can think of, Mr. Pierpont?"

"No. I'm afraid not."

Longstreet closed his notepad. "We'll be at the U.P. Hotel if anything comes to mind."

Outside Cane led the way down Sixteenth Street toward the depot.

"What do you make of it?" Longstreet asked.

"Damn clever."

"You're right about them striking again. We need to get word to Colonel Crook."

"There'll be a Western Union office at the depot. We can send a wire there. The colonel can notify the league to be on the lookout for counterfeit bonds and a beautiful woman who passes them."

"She may not be working alone."

"Probably isn't."

"Then what do we do?"

"We wait."

Longstreet lifted a brow. "Wait?"

"I haven't been at this much longer than you, Beau; but one thing the colonel's made me believe is the value of information. Trains follow tracks. They don't leave any. We need this woman to tell us where to look for her."

The Cheyenne Depot was a stair-stepped

clapboard structure. The original station now housed the post office and a Western Union office. A larger station had been added on with ticket counters, passenger lounge, and dining room. The most recent addition, the U.P. Hotel, climbed the skyline east of the two older structures.

Longstreet waited at a window while Cane telegraphed Cecile St. James's description and other pertinent facts of the case to Colonel Crook. He watched an arriving westbound train discharge passengers and freight. *Speaking of beautiful women,* he picked the dark-haired beauty out of the arriving passenger crowd. His gaze followed her across the platform to the U.P. Hotel. *Now that would be a painless way to await further developments.*

Chicago

The Counselor waded through the swirling bluster blowing off the lake among the buildings along Michigan Avenue. He turned north away from the stench of the stockyards to the stone-edifice monument to the constancy of the U.S. Postal Service. He climbed broad steps to an arched entry portal guarded by a life-size pair of gilt lions. The service counter flanked a massive lobby whose far wall presented row upon row of locked boxes. He fished a small key from his vest pocket and unlocked his box. He withdrew a single envelope, relocked the box, and went to a counter set aside for private business.

He tore the envelope open to find a money order in the amount of eighty thousand dollars. The wheels were in motion. He drew a new envelope from his case and addressed it to a blind trust held at Salmon Chase Bank of New York on behalf of a shell corporation, having a note payable to one Jay Gould in the amount of one million dollars. He inserted the money order and posted it at the service desk.

U.P. Hotel
Cheyenne
Kingsley stepped off the stage in Cheyenne and made his way to the U.P. Hotel. The registration desk stood across a spacious yet spartan lobby. He was greeted with a note.

Cheyenne Union Bank, 2:00 PM.
— Maples

He checked his pocket watch. Time enough for a quick bite of lunch in the station dining room. After lunch he made his way uptown to the bank, arriving moments before two.

"Mr. Kingsley?"

A shapely dark-eyed beauty with cultured manners took him by surprise.

"Yes."

"Samantha Maples." She extended her hand.

Still it took a moment to register. "Agent Maples?"

She smiled with anticipated amusement. "You were expecting someone else?"

"Why, ah, I mean."

"Don't be. It happens all the time. Mr. Pinkerton thinks it a disarming advantage."

"Disarming, I see, quite so."

"I expect that gentleman seated near the vault is the cashier. Come along."

He fell in step beside her still trying to make sense of his new partner.

"Mr. Pierpont?"

He looked puzzled. "Yes."

"Samantha Maples, Pinkerton Agency, this is my associate, Reginald Kingsley. We've come about the Texas & Pacific bond you accepted. We are retained by Texas & Pacific to investigate the matter. May we have a few moments of your time?"

"Why, ah." He cut his eyes to Kingsley as if the man might provide some sense to what he'd just heard.

"It shouldn't take long," Kingsley said. "Please, have a seat."

She arranged her skirts, opened her handbag, and drew out a pad and pencil. Kingsley noted a pearl-handled revolver in the bag. *Remarkable, and no doubt she knows how to use it.*

"Now, Mr. Pierpont, can you tell us what happened?"

"Certainly."

The man had regained his composure.

"But first may I ask how you know my name? We made no report to Pinkerton."

"You sign the bank statements as cashier. Now, about the bond."

"As I told Mr. Longstreet and his associate Mr. Cane, the bond was used to secure a letter of credit for a woman calling herself Cecile St. James."

"Longstreet? That name is familiar."

"Formerly one of ours," Kingsley said. "He's recently gone over to the Great Western Detective League. Cane is one of theirs."

Samantha bit a thoughtful lip. "I'm not familiar with that organization."

"The bank has retained Colonel Crook's organization to help recover our loss," Pierpont said.

"Then perhaps we shall have some help?"

76

"Not exactly, it takes some explaining," Kingsley said.

"Continue, Mr. Pierpont."

An hour later they left the bank for the stroll back to the depot hotel.

"I say, what do you make of all that?" Kingsley said.

"It's the opening act to the play."

"Opening act? I've been given to understand the first bond was presented in Chicago."

"Not related to this play."

"What do you mean?"

"The Chicago bond was redeemed by an amateur opportunist, the son of an engraver who was murdered. He found the bond following his father's death. We believe the engraver was holding out on whoever paid him to forge the bonds. Whoever that is killed him to cover their tracks. What we have here is the passing of the perpetrator's first bond."

"So you believe there will be others."

"Almost certainly. Creating the plate for a decent counterfeit is an arduous and expensive task. Why would anyone go to that kind of trouble and stop at one impression? No, there will be more. The pertinent questions are where and when?"

"Well, it is plain we don't have much to go on. Thousands of women could fit the description Pierpont gave us."

"I'm afraid we'll have to wait until we get another report to give our search some direction."

"Quite so," Kingsley said.

"I intend to wait here. With access to the railroad, chances are I'll be in position to move quickly the next time a bond is cashed. There's no point to you twiddling your thumbs here."

"No, I think not. I shall return to Denver on the morning stage."

CHAPTER EIGHT

Rawlins

The westbound train slowly rolled into the station, spewing clouds of steam and throaty whistle tones. Outside the streaked window glass, a dusty frontier tapestry scrolled by. The town appeared to be little more than one street stretched along the tracks across from the depot. She could easily pick out the small hotel from her seat. She'd meet her employer's rat-faced man there and be done with this dump in a day or two at the worst. The train lurched to a stop, hissing steam and squealing brakes. She collected her traveling case and started up the coach aisle for the door.

The smell assaulted her senses as she stepped down to the platform. *What on earth?* A mocking chorus bleated response to the question. Sheep, lots of them, filled the air with dust and noise and unbearable stench. She clutched a lace handkerchief to her nose, glanced across the tracks to the stock pens, and hurried off in the opposite direction toward town. She reached the small hotel lobby to the horrifying re-alization. *She'd been followed by fragrance Eau de ewe.*

She coughed into her handkerchief.

"May I be of assistance?"

The desk clerk eyed her with something more than mild interest. She'd become used to having an ogling effect on men. This one had slick dark hair parted in the middle, a waxed mustache, and leering gaze that exposed carnal interest. The prospect re-pulsed her imagination, near matching her disgust at the sheep stench. The oily voyeur could be brushed aside or toyed with at her pleasure. The sheep smell could not.

"Does one ever get used to it?"

"Used to it? Ah, you mean the sweet scent of prosperity? One adapts. Now, how may I help you Miss . . . ?"

"Cecile, Cecile Carroll. I shall need a room."

"And how long will you be staying with us, Miss Carroll? It is Miss Carroll, isn't it?"

"It is and to be blunt, no longer than necessary."

"Pity. That will be a dollar a night."

She passed a dollar across the counter and signed the guest register. "I should like to leave a message for a Señor Escobar who may be checking in later."

"He has already arrived. I can deliver your message to him."

"Thank you." She scratched a note. *Meet in the lobby for supper at six.*

She found Escobar waiting in the lobby. The man had a menace about him she found uncomfortable. Uncomfortable as it may be, she could overlook it given the money she stood to make for a few weeks suffering an association with him. He nodded an unspoken greeting. She led the way out to the boardwalk.

"There's a café down the street. I doubt there are many to choose from in this town."

He nodded.

The Ram's Head Café was small. The smell of freshly baked bread mercifully muted the less than pleasant street odor. She chose a corner table far enough away from the only other diners that they might have a quiet conversation. She withdrew the Laramie Cattleman's Bank letter of credit from her handbag and passed it across the table. Escobar placed it in his coat pocket without looking.

"I take it you had no difficulty," he said.

She shook her head.

A harried waiter approached the table. "May I take your order?"

"Do you have a special?" she asked.

"Mutton."

She wrinkled her nose. "Of course. Anything else?"

"Fried chicken."

"I'll have that."

"I'll have the mutton," Escobar said.

The waiter went off.

"You will obtain another letter tomorrow?"

"Yes. I'm out of this disgusting town on the next train after that."

"Sí. I will meet you in Green River the day after tomorrow. How long will it be before the authorities know of our activities?"

She shrugged. "They may know by now. If not, they soon will. The important thing is to keep moving."

The waiter arrived with two steaming plates.

Escobar wolfed at his.

Cecile picked at hers.

The pocked man pointed his fork, "How is the chicken?"

"Tastes like mutton."

The Herder's Bank of Rawlins was small and sleepy. It had its share of sweet scent, but without much prosperity to go with it. The waxy thin banker with slicked back hair looked as though he might have been equally comfortable serving as an undertaker or dealing faro. She disarmed him with a smile, dazzled him with a bond, and caught the afternoon train west with a letter of credit in hand.

U.P. Hotel
Cheyenne
The dark-haired woman with the catch-your-eye figure floated across the lobby. Longstreet didn't hesitate. He managed to casually meet her at the dining room entry. He paused with a slight bow.

"After you, ma'am."

"Why thank you, sir. There is something chivalrous about a southern gentleman."

"Beauregard Longstreet at your service."

"Ah, Mr. Longstreet, I heard you were in town."

"You heard I was in town? Who would have told you such a thing? I've only recently arrived and scarcely knew it myself."

She smiled an even white sparkle. "Reginald Kingsley."

"His Lordship is here?"

"His Lordship?"

"Private joke." He looked about the lobby. "Is he here?"

"He left."

"Are you Pinkerton?"

"I am. Samantha Maples." She extended her hand.

Longstreet accepted it. "I was about to have a bite of supper, would you care to join me?"

She looked him up and down with an amused half smile. "Why, yes, I believe I should enjoy that."

A waiter in a starched jacket led them to a candlelit corner table set in linen, china, crystal, and silver. Longstreet made a show of holding her chair.

"May I bring you something to drink?"

A flicker of mischief crossed her eye. "I believe I shall have a sherry."

"And you, sir?"

He knit his brow and thought about a whiskey. "I'll have one too."

"Kingsley tells me you were once one of us, Mr. Longstreet."

"I was. Please call me Beau, all my friends do."

"I'm sure they do. Very well then, Beau, you must call me Sam. Only my best friends call me that. I enjoy the social ruffle it causes the prim and proper."

The waiter returned with their drinks.

Longstreet lifted his glass, "To social ruffle, then."

She laughed a throaty laugh and returned his toast.

"And what may I offer you this evening?" the waiter asked.

"I believe I'll have a steak," Samantha said.

"Make that two."

The waiter bustled off to the kitchen.

"So you left the Pinkerton Agency for some detective league or other as Kingsley tells it. Why?"

"Money. What's more interesting than that is how you came to be a Pinkerton."

"Well, I suppose that was money too, after a fashion. I came west from Boston. Got as far as Chicago and decided I needed a job. By chance I met William Pinkerton. He suggested I apply at his agency."

"Did you have experience as an investigator?"

"Heavens no, women are not common in this business or hadn't you noticed?"

"I had. That's why I asked. So old Pinkerton saw some potential in you?"

She struck that mischievous pose again. "I suppose he did. Men sometimes do."

"I'm sure they do."

She smiled. "Some of them are criminal. William saw advantages to a woman operative. Some criminals are women, take the case at hand for example. I doubt the lady with the bogus bonds anticipates being pursued by a woman. Societal expectations can be useful in that regard, don't you think?"

"It would seem so. My own are a bit wobbly at the moment."

"Good," she said with a mysterious twinkle in her eye.

Longstreet couldn't tell disarmed from undressed. Well, of course he could; it's just, at the moment, he felt a bit of both.

The waiter arrived with the steaks.

By the time they finished dessert and a nightcap in the lounge, they'd tippled enough sherry to make the climb upstairs something less than steady. Ever the gentleman, Longstreet steadied Samantha's arm to her door. She fumbled in her purse for the key. She concentrated on the lock. Longstreet guided her hand. The key found its way home. The door clicked open. She turned, flushing dreamy eyes to her escort.

"Thank you, Beau. It was a lovely evening."

He bent to her upturned lips. Soft and sweet flashed white light.

She grasped him by the lapels and dragged him into the darkened room. The door clicked closed.

A message slipped under the door went unnoticed in the flurry.

She awoke to the distant sound of a train whistle. Gray morning light filtered through lace curtains. Beau slept undisturbed beside her. Her head felt a bit fuzzy. She reckoned it a small price for the pleasant echoes of all that came with it. She lifted the sheet in recollection, magnificent, truly magnificent. She glanced around the room at the discarded reminders of the rush. The message caught her eye. She slipped out of bed, careful not to wake him, and padded across the room. She picked up the envelope and read.

Texas & Pacific reports a bond redeemed Cattleman's Bank, Laramie.

— Kingsley

She glanced at Longstreet. *Pity.* She bent to gather her clothes.

■ ■ ■ ■

Daylight intruded on his private reserve of fatigue and fog. He pushed it aside in favor of more pleasant reflections. Then it dawned. She was gone. He sat up. So were her bag and clothes. She was gone all right. Where?

Shady Grove

The colonel's head nodded. I shook a writer's cramp out of my hand and closed my notebook. We'd covered rather a lot of ground already this week.

His head bobbed. "Sorry about that, Robert. I may have dozed off there for a moment. Now, then, where were we?"

"Longstreet and Samantha Maples had just gotten, ah, acquainted."

He smiled. "One of Longstreet's many talents. I quite admired him for that."

"He does seem to have women fall into his arms at the drop of a hat."

"Unlike you, my young friend, who must be pushed by my more assertive nature."

"Unlike Longstreet, I'm more than content with my lot in that respect."

"Lot is it? I shouldn't let her hear you refer to her in such plebian terms."

"What plebian terms?" Penny said.

She couldn't have arrived at a more inopportune moment.

"The colonel and I were discussing Longstreet's proclivity for attracting women and I was telling him how happy I am."

She lifted a brow that seemed to question the veracity of my explanation. "And those are plebian terms?"

"I didn't think so."

"And you, Colonel, what did you find plebian in them?"

He held up a hand in protest. "Most likely a poor choice of words on my part. I thought he might have been more extravagant in singing your praise is all I meant to say."

"Really? I shouldn't have thought you'd admit to a foible like a poor choice of words."

"It must be time for my nap. Until next week then, Robert, enjoy your lot in life."

She knit her brow, puzzled, and pushed him off down the hall.

I'd have to explain it all later. It was only a question of *how*.

CHAPTER NINE

Laramie

Edwin Sinclair's fat fingers trembled as he stared at the wire from the Salmon Chase Bank of New York. *Counterfeit?* He'd placed one hundred thousand dollars of bank funds at risk on a counterfeit bond. A loss that size could put the bank at risk. How could he have been taken in so easily? A Texas & Pacific Railroad bond was as good as gold. In this case clearly it was not. He'd never thought to question it. He couldn't bring himself to admit he'd been charmed. He remembered the classically beautiful woman with the cultured manners and a come-hither flicker in her eye. He fancied he'd imagined that at the time. The look was come-hither all right but not for the purpose he might have imagined. *Now what?* He had no idea. He could report it to Sheriff Bisbee, but what could he do? The woman was obviously long gone. Still the loss must be reported. Whatever measures might be taken must be taken. He rose from his desk and crossed the lobby to the head teller's cage.

"I'm going to see the sheriff, Mable. I should be back before closing."

She nodded a look of concern. "Is everything all right, sir?"

"Fine, everything's fine."

She watched him go. *Fine* seldom necessitated a visit to the sheriff.

Laramie Sheriff Trent Bisbee sensed alarm the moment Edwin Sinclair entered the office.

"Is everything all right, Ed? You look as though the bank has been robbed."

"I suppose it has, after a fashion."

"What?"

"Here, read this." He handed the telegram across the sheriff's cluttered desk and collapsed into a barrel-backed side chair.

Counterfeit, the word leaped from the page. The sheriff shook his head. "Don't tell me. The bond was in the amount of one hundred thousand dollars."

The banker's jaw dropped. "Why, yes, how did you know?"

"I received this just this morning." He rummaged through a stack of dodgers on his desk to produce a telegram he handed to Sinclair.

The wire was an alert to Great Western Detective League members in regard to a counterfeit ring obtaining letters of credit secured by Texas & Pacific Railroad bonds.

"I was about to come by this afternoon to alert you to the problem."

"Sadly it would have been weeks too late. The question is, what's to be done now?"

"The Great Western Detective League is on the case. I shall report your loss to Colonel Crook. He will coordinate the investigation among other league members."

"Great Western Detective League, what's that?"

"It's an association of law enforcement officers across the west that cooperate in solving cases that cross jurisdictions. Other losses from this ring have already been reported. That means there is a trail of sorts. Quite often the exchange of information among league members leads to the apprehension of criminals like these. What can you tell me about the person who gave you this bond?"

U.P. Hotel
Cane crossed the lobby from the dinning room. The desk clerk waved a Western

Union wire.

"Mr. Cane, I was about to run this up to your room."

Cane tore it open and read.

Bond reported at Laramie Cattleman's Bank.
Proceed a pace thitherward.

— Crook

"Is Mr. Longstreet in?"

"I believe he is, sir, room 203."

Cane took the stairs to the second floor two at a time. He knocked at the door at the head of the stairs.

"Coming." Footfalls followed the muffled response. The door swung open. Longstreet blinked sleepy-eyed, dressed in britches and braces.

"Bad night?" Cane handed him the telegram. "If we hurry we can catch the noon train."

"Give me ten minutes."

"Meet me in the lobby."

They left the muted glow of the lobby for the bright morning bustle of Sixteenth Street. Cane led the way west to the depot.

"I've got a hunch," Cane said.

"What's that?"

"They're following the railroad west."

"Could be, what do we do?"

"You go to Laramie to find out what happened."

"And you?"

"I go to Rawlins to see what might happen next."

Laramie

Longstreet gazed out the window as the train slowed. Two throaty hoots announced Laramie Station. He gathered his traveling case.

"If you need to reach me, wire the Western Union office in Rawlins," Cane said.

Longstreet nodded to the window across the aisle and the two-story clapboard building beyond. "You can reach me at the Laramie Hotel."

He headed up the aisle to the car door. He stepped off the platform and started up the short block walk to the hotel. The hotel desk clerk checked him into room 202 and directed him across the street and up the block to the Cattleman's Bank. He dropped his valise in the room and made it to the bank just before closing.

The portly banker with bushy white muttonchops introduced himself as Edwin Sinclair. He recounted a familiar story they'd already heard in Cheyenne.

"Sorry I can't be more helpful, Mr. Longstreet. You'll forgive me if I take some comfort from all the investigative interest in our loss."

"Oh? What interest?"

"Well, yourself of course and the Pinkerton agency was here a few days ago."

"Pinkerton?"

"Yes, though I must say I thought their approach somewhat unusual."

"Unusual, how so?"

He lowered his voice to a confidential tone. "The Pinkerton agent was *a woman.*"

"Samantha Maples."

"Why, yes, how did you know?"

"Let's just say I've made her acquaintance."

The desk clerk glanced up as Longstreet approached the counter.

"Are you finding everything to your satisfaction, sir?"

He nodded. "Is Miss Maples in?"

"I'm sorry, sir. I don't know and if I did I shouldn't be at liberty to say."

"I see. Perhaps you would be kind enough to deliver a message to her."

"Certainly, sir."

Longstreet scratched a note

95

Dinner at six?
Meet in the lobby.

— Beau

He folded the slip, handed it to the clerk, and went to his room.

Six O'Clock

She swept down the steps to the lobby, the picture of modesty in a plain gray traveling gown that fit her to exquisite effect. Longstreet waited, holding an expression intended to give nothing away. She smiled the disarming smile of one caught in a mild deception.

She crossed the lobby and patted his cheek. "Beau Longstreet, what a pleasant surprise. What brings you to Laramie?"

"You forgot to say goodbye."

"Urgent message and you were sleeping so peacefully. I'm sure you understand. What brings you to Laramie?"

"I'm sure you know."

She lowered dark lashes. "You have the advantage of me."

"I doubt that. Urgent message, you understand."

She smiled at a bit of innuendo. "I do. And I must say I'm pleased you are here. It puts a fresh light on this frightfully dreary

96

little town. Now, are we going to have a drink and some supper or are we going to stand here and listen to our stomachs growl?"

He offered his arm. "I'm told the café next door is passably good."

"Now there's a ringing endorsement if I ever heard one."

"You're the one who said 'dreary.' "

She squeezed his arm. "I suppose I shouldn't, but for some reason I find you amusing."

"Irresistible charm."

"Yes, of course, that must be it."

Denver

Penny's shift ended at three o'clock that Saturday. I walked her home with a stop for an ice cream sundae. Nothing like a little caramel and fudge to smooth over a rough spot that could scarcely be explained by saying, "it's just the colonel being the colonel," whether it was true or not. I let the caramel sweeten her mood and prudently changed the subject.

"It's finished."

Her expression registered an uncertainty that bespoke somewhat more than curiosity.

"What's finished?"

"The book, the Sam Bass book."

Her expression softened. "That's wonderful. What do you plan to do now?"

"I'm submitting it to a publishing house in New York."

"That's so exciting, Robert. They'll publish it then?"

"I hope so."

"Oh, Robert, they will. I know they will."

"Thank you. I appreciate your confidence. I hope you're right."

We exchanged spoonfuls of sundae, Penny getting a taste of my fudge and she giving me a taste of her caramel. It was a little ritual we did most sundae times. To me in some symbolic way it made a metaphor of us. The combined tastes more savory than either alone. I could imagine. We did it more owing to the fact that she liked it than to my imaginings. Those dreams I thought best left to my private yearnings.

"They've made a moving picture show of Mr. Twain's book *Tom Sawyer.* It's showing at the Bijou. Would you care to see the matinee tomorrow?"

She nodded for another spoon of fudge.

"Robert, wouldn't it be ever so grand if one day they made a moving picture of your book?"

"It would be grand, but let's not put our cart so far ahead of the horse."

"Is it, Robert?"

"Is it what?"

"Our cart?"

I felt my face warm. *Our cart,* I'd said it to be sure without thinking the implication. There was the question. *Was it?* It seemed it must. "It is."

She took my hands in hers and gave her Mona Lisa a rosy glow.

"For the moment let's see how moving pictures treat Mr. Twain's cart."

She laughed that throaty mischievous laugh of hers.

CHAPTER TEN

Rawlins

Cane stepped off the train to the depot platform in the gathering gloom of early evening. The evening breeze struck him full in the face. *Sheep! Why would anyone put up with such a foul-smelling business?* He could think of far better ways to make a living than husbanding stinking woolies with their dips and urine and musty shearing. A porter handling freight directed him up the street to the hotel. He found a room, some supper, and an early night.

Cane arrived at the Herder's Bank of Rawlins the next morning as a birdlike banker with pomade hair, waxed mustache, and dark suit turned the window sign to open promptly at nine o'clock. He waited for the banker to unlatch the front door and stepped inside.

"Good morning, Travis McCreedy." He

extended a hand. "How may we be of assistance?"

"Briscoe Cane, Great Western Detective League. I'm here about a bond."

"A bond?"

"A Texas & Pacific Railroad bond, likely in the amount of one hundred thousand dollars."

The banker's thin brows lifted in recognition.

"You've seen one then."

He nodded, sensing something amiss. "Detective league you said?"

Cane nodded.

"Perhaps we should have a seat at my desk." He led the way across the sun-splashed polished lobby floor to a desk beside the vault.

"Please have a seat."

Cane took the offered chair. McCreedy steepled his fingers.

"Is the bond stolen?"

"We are following the trail of a woman who uses them to arrange letters of credit."

"A woman."

"Has she been here?"

"Yes."

"Did you provide her a letter of credit?"

"As a matter of fact we did. A Texas & Pacific bond is an impeccable security."

"I'm sure it is, unless it's forged."

The banker's eyes shot round.

"Do you still have the bond?"

He nodded.

"May I see it?"

The man got to his feet ashen-faced and went to the vault. He handed it across the desk, his hand shaking noticeably.

"May I have this?"

"Are you sure this one is forged?"

"The paying agent is Salmon Chase in New York. You can wire the cashier there if you like. He's familiar with the circumstances surrounding these. I can come back for it tomorrow if you prefer."

"Yes, please."

Escobar stroked the thin line of dark beard at his chin. He watched the tall, lean stranger. He'd happened by the bank that morning and became curious over the early arriving customer. When the banker went to the vault to retrieve what looked like the bond, his suspicions grew stronger. Someone was on to them. The banker would soon discover the letter of credit had been cashed.

The stranger stood to shake the banker's hand. Escobar crossed the street and picked out a shop window to study. He watched the stranger leave the bank in the window reflection. The man crossed the street. Escobar watched his reflection mount the boardwalk off to his right and turn in the direction of the depot. Escobar watched out of the corner of his eye. He gave him a half-block start before following along behind.

Cane went to the Western Union desk at the depot. He scratched out a wire to Longstreet.

She's moving west along the U.P. line.
Evanston and Green River are next.
You take Evanston.
> — *Cane*

Escobar approached the Western Union counter. He made a show of examining the train schedule, listening to the stranger at the nearby ticket counter buy a ticket for Green River. He cocked an ear as the Western Union telegrapher tapped his key. The stranger was definitely on to them. More than that, he did not work alone. He stepped up to the Western Union counter and wrote his own short message.

Green River
A soft rap at the door lifted the lacy veil of sleep. The room resolved golden in late

afternoon sun. Satisfied at having obtained yet another letter of credit from the Boatman's Bank of Green River that morning, she'd dozed off counting the sums she'd collected in this little caper. She fell asleep in the comfort of knowing there was more where that came from.

"Who is it?"

"Telegram for Miss Antoine." The raspy voice declared adolescent male.

Cecile glanced at the gown tossed over a chair weighing the effort to make herself decent. "Leave it under the door."

A yellow foolscap slipped under the door. No footfalls departed beyond the door. The lad waited. She rewarded him with squeaking bedsprings as she fumbled in her purse for a coin. She rose, slid it under the door, and picked up the telegram as the messenger retreated down the hall. She sat on the bed and slit the envelope with a fingernail. The message could scarcely be more cryptic.

Move on.

— E.

The change in plans suggested something may be afoot. She'd known all along it was only a matter of time before the authorities caught on to the scheme. She'd hoped for more time before the need to take evasive steps arose. She eyed her gown. Oh bother, Evanston tomorrow. She lay back to the complaint of the bedsprings and drifted off to rest for supper.

Chicago

The Counselor hurried along Michigan Avenue, braced by a strong southwesterly breeze laden with stockyard scent. On days like today he found the city offensively agrarian. He mopped a light sheen of perspiration from his forehead with a handkerchief as he climbed the stone steps to the post office. He checked the post box every few days now that his client's program was in operation. Today the box yielded a second payment order. He crossed the sun-soaked marble floor to a counter set aside for preparing postings. He opened a battered leather case, drew out a plain brown envelope, and transferred the payment order to it. He turned to the service counter, slid the parcel to the postal clerk, paid the postage, and left. The transfer completed in less than five minutes. *Two down, ten to go.*

Green River

By the time Cane reached Green River the

following day, the Boatman's Bank had closed. The sleepy little river town owed its existence to providing a junction for river commerce and the railroad. Eastbound and westbound passengers and drayage found their way upstream and downstream from the combined rail station and river port. Throw in the teamsters who assisted the barge traffic and the town had a commercial life of its own. Cane took a room at the hotel, never noticing the dark-skinned man with pockmarked, hawk-sharp features watching him from afar.

Escobar waited for the investigator to check into the hotel. He watched while he climbed the stairs to his room. At the registration counter he took a room for himself noting the last guest to register, one Briscoe Cane, could be found in room 207. He let himself in to a room on the third floor and puzzled over the problem of what to do about their pursuer.

Assuming Cecile had done her work before leaving town, this Briscoe Cane would find another banker with another bogus bond. He'd come to Green River with no obvious clue, unless he'd guessed they were following the Union Pacific rail route. If he had, he'd be off to Evanston as soon as he left the bank. He needed to slow him down, but how? He ruled out gun play, too great a risk of being caught. He fingered his blade. He'd have to get close. The man looked old. Still he had a competence about him. Men didn't stay in this line of work past the time they could acquit themselves satisfactorily. Any that did, didn't last long. This one did not strike him as the type. No, in close quarters, anything could happen. He needed something unexpected. He needed an accident, fatal if possible, debilitating at the very least. He stroked his mustache and nodded slowly. It was a long shot, but it might provide exactly what he needed.

CHAPTER ELEVEN

The Shoshone came down from the Wind River country to trade with the river men. Escobar noticed the camp east of town when the train rolled in. It was a short walk out of town to their clustered lodges. Camp dogs announced his arrival. He signed his desire to trade to the young man who greeted him. The young man thought the request strange, but led the white man to the lodge of a shaman who might assist him.

The shaman, Winter Grass, greeted the scarred one at his lodge. He listened to the man's request. The man did not offer trade goods. He offered gold coins that might be used to buy goods from the river men. He accepted the man's offer.

"Return at sunset."

Three hours later Escobar found the shaman sitting at his lodge fire; a leather sack secured with a thong rested beside him.

Escobar paid twenty dollars in gold pieces,

accepted the sack, and disappeared in the gathering gloom.

Evanston

Longstreet stepped out of Essex House to the boardwalk fronting the hotel. The hollow in his belly reminded him that it had been a long time since a light breakfast early that morning. He looked up and down the street searching the blue evening shadows for the likely sign of a restaurant. He didn't see any obvious choices, but he did see a fine figure of a woman half a block west. Oh well, he had to go somewhere. He strolled along behind her dividing his attention between the need of a meal and the sway of her hips.

She paused in the middle of the next block to admire something in the window of a storefront. As he approached he could see she was reading a menu.

"Anything look good?"

She glanced over her shoulder. Appraising hazel eyes glistened in window light. He smiled.

"As a matter of fact."

"Something special?"

"One never knows before one tries." She smiled, her complexion cream. She stepped aside to let him read.

"Roast beef."

"I might have guessed."

"Really. That obvious?"

"It is."

"And you?"

"Petite portion."

"I might have guessed."

"Touché."

"Shall we?"

"We've not been formally introduced."

"My apologies, Beauregard Longstreet at your service." He made a slight bow.

Cecile thought quickly. "Cora Collier, Mr. Longstreet."

"My friends call me, Beau, Miss Collier."

"I'm sure they do. How do you know it's miss?"

"Oh, I beg your pardon, Mrs. Collier." He looked at his shoes. "I meant no harm."

A musical laugh caught somewhere at the back of her throat. "Miss it is, if it matters."

He chuckled, raising his hands in surrender. "Shall we then?"

"I thought you'd never ask."

He held the door. A waiter in a starched apron led them to a candlelit corner table. The waiter held her chair.

"May I offer you a beverage?"

Longstreet deferred to Cora Collier.

"Do you have a sherry?"

The waiter nodded.

"Make that two."

"Very good, sir."

She tilted the point of her chin and lowered long lashes over those crystalline eyes. "Longstreet, a rather distinguished name in the south, isn't it?"

"That would be my cousin's doing."

"Did you also serve?"

"I did."

The waiter returned with their drinks. "May I take your order, ma'am?"

A twinkle crossed her eye. "He'll have the roast beef special and I'll have a petite portion."

"Very good."

Longstreet lifted his glass. "Suddenly I feel rather useless."

She lifted hers. "That remains to be seen."

They toasted.

"Do you live in Evanston?"

She shook her head. "I have family in the Wind River country. I'm on my way to visit them. What brings you to Evanston, Beau?"

"Business."

"What sort of business?"

"I'm a private investigator."

"Oh, my, that sounds exciting. Are you with the Pinkerton Agency?"

"I was. I now represent the Great Western

Detective League."

She knit her brow. "Can't say I've ever heard of that."

"We prefer it that way."

"I see. What sort of nefarious activity brings you to Evanston? It seems a rather sleepy little place for such mischief."

"Bank fraud."

"That does sound sinister." *And too close for comfort. Pity.*

The waiter returned with steaming plates.

Longstreet drained his glass. "Care for another?"

She nodded.

"Bring us the bottle."

By the time they finished the apple pie and sherry, Cora Collier had a rosy glow on her golden complexion. She took his arm for the short walk back to the hotel.

"May I walk you to your room?"

She lifted her eyes to his. "A most gentle-manly offer, Beau Longstreet, but perhaps it might serve propriety if I found my own way this time." She patted his cheek. "Until then." She turned and climbed the stairs.

Longstreet watched her go. He shook his head. *Until when?*

Cane returned to his room after supper. He was tired after a long day on the train. He lit the bedside lamp and poured water into the basin from a pitcher on the small dresser. He splashed water on his face and dried it on a towel. He hung his gun belt over the back of a chair and draped his coat over it. He tossed his backup Forehand & Wadsworth Bull Dog on the nightstand next to the lamp. He kicked off his boots and britches and took off his ribbon tie and shirt. Down to his long-handles he pulled back the bed cover and tested the springs to a welcoming squeak. He huffed out the lamp and stretched out, his body heavy with fatigue.

Dark eyes glittered black light. A tongue tasted the scent of water in the air. Brown markings edged in black spread a pattern over the diminutive length of gray coils. The dusty rattler, smallest of all rattlesnakes, is a rare breed native to the Green River formation. Boasting the most potent venom of the species, this serpent ideally suited the assassin's purpose. It slithered forward from the safety of the corner beneath the bed.

Sleep tugged at Cane's eyelids. He drifted off. A soft sliding sound intruded somewhere at the back of his subconscious. He snapped alert, listening.

He'd imagined it.

No, there it is again.

Something lightly brushed the foot of the bed, *a rat?*

It moved again. The barest whisper of sound, a faint sensation climbed the bedpost toward his right foot. *Rats don't climb posts!*

He reached for the nightstand, fumbling in the dark for a lucifer. He found one. He transferred it to his left hand and reached out again, groping for the Bull Dog.

The bedpost betrayed movement again.

He waited.

Movement stopped.

He flicked the match. Sulfur light flared. Bright eyes glittered. The Bull Dog barked muzzle flash and powder smoke.

Cane rolled out of bed and lit the lamp as the hallway beyond the door exploded with hotel guests reacting to a gunshot reverberating down the hall in the middle of the night.

He held up the lamp. The shattered snake lay on the floor at the wall across from the foot of the bed; twisting in spasmodic reflex it went still. Not just any snake, a dusty rattler. His knees took on water after the fact. *What the hell is a dusty rattler doing here?*

"Mr. Cane, Mr. Cane!" The night clerk

pounded the door.

Cane opened it.

"What happened? Is everything all right?"

He swung the door wide and held the lamp to light the dead snake.

"Oh my! I'm dreadfully sorry. I've no idea how this might have happened." He stepped back into the hall. "Go back to your rooms, folks. Just an accident. No harm done. Sorry you've been disturbed."

The following morning mood of the Boatman's Bank cashier matched the dreary gray drizzle. He'd already issued a letter of credit to a woman who was certainly long gone. *Too late again!* Cane seethed. Then there was the matter of the snake in his hotel room. Not just any snake mind you, the most deadly venomous snake in the territory. In his room. On the second floor. *Coincidence?* Stranger things have happened. *Too much to credit to coincidence, the woman isn't working alone.*

Evanston

Longstreet opened the bank the next morning. The cashier returned a blank stare when he inquired about a Texas & Pacific Railroad bond in the amount of one hundred thousand dollars. The man was certain he hadn't seen one of those. He warned the banker to be on the lookout for anyone approaching him with a bond like that. He agreed to contact Longstreet at Essex House should anyone make such an attempt.

Longstreet pondered this turn of events on the short walk back to the hotel. Something wasn't right. The pattern fit. Where was she? Is it possible he got to Evanston before she did? That seemed unlikely, but possible. He was still mulling the puzzle when he reached the lobby desk.

"May I help you, sir?" The clerk blinked owlishly behind spectacles drifted down the bridge of a beaklike nose.

"I'd like to leave a message for a guest."

"Certainly, sir." The clerk slid paper and pencil across the counter.

It was a wonderful evening last. Would you care to join me for lunch?

— Beau

He folded the paper, wrote her name on the blank side, and passed it to the clerk.

"Cora Collier," the clerk said as he knit his brow. "I'm sorry, sir, we don't have anyone registered by that name."

"Are you sure? We had dinner last night. She was staying here then."

The clerk shook his head, running a finger down the register.

"She's an attractive woman, chestnut hair, hazel eyes."

"That could be Miss Antoine, but she checked out early this morning."

"Miss Antoine?"

"Cecile Antoine, she spent a couple of days with us."

Why would she use an alias? Unless . . . What was he thinking?

Later that morning a swarthy man with a pockmarked face wearing a black suit approached the registration desk.

"May I help you, sir?"

"I need a room."

He spun the register for the stranger to sign.

"Very good, Mr. Escobar, that will be a dollar." He turned to a board with the available room keys. "Let me see, ah, we have a message for you." He slid the paper across the counter.

Escobar read.

Meet me in North Platte.

— C

North Platte? Why double back east? To

break the pattern. The problem must be bigger than the man in Green River. He turned on his heel and strode toward the door.

"Sir, what about your room?"

The stranger never looked back.

CHAPTER TWELVE

Denver

The moving picture show gave Mr. Twain's *Tom Sawyer* a passing portrayal, though much of the depth and feeling was sacrificed on the altar of brevity. We partook an early supper and I walked Penny home in the stillness of a mild spring evening. We sat on the front porch, listening to cricket songs as we watched the stars come out.

"Did you enjoy the moving picture show?"

She tilted her chin eye to eye. "I did. I tried to imagine your name scrolling by in the credits."

I felt my cheeks warm. "There goes that runaway cart again."

"I can dream. We can dream. You said it's our cart."

I slipped an arm around her shoulder and pulled her close. "It does feel better when you're in it. The cart I mean." She turned her lips to mine. I took them softly at first. I felt her shiver. The porch swing groaned. Wild imaginings exploded in my mind's eye and elsewhere. We rocked. The swing made little sounds at the back of her throat. We gasped for a breath.

"Oh, Robert, the cart, I'm afraid it is running away."

I drew on the lines, holding her still. "I shouldn't allow my feelings to become so bold."

"And I shouldn't allow myself to be so willing, except . . ."

"Except what?"

"I like it."

I kissed her again, more chastely this time. A question gnawed at me all the long walk home. *What would Beau Longstreet do?*

Laramie

Samantha drummed her fingers on the small side table as she gazed out the yellowed lace curtains covering her hotel room window. The dusty street below baked in late afternoon sun. Commerce slowed to a plodding pace in the shimmering heat. She hated waiting. Time crawled. It might have been entertaining if Longstreet were still here. He had a certain, *irresistible charm*? That was one way to describe it. The handsome southerner made for a rather more pleasant pastime. He'd disappeared as suddenly as she had in Cheyenne. Where had he gone? It stood to reason the Great Western Detective League had a lead the Pinkerton Agency did not. And so she had nothing further to do but wait. Wait for what? At this point it seemed she waited for little more than the next drop of sweat to trickle down the cleft between her breasts.

A muffled knock at the door broke the monotony.

"Telegram, Miss Maples."

She got up from the table and rummaged in her purse for a quarter. She crossed the room in three strides and cracked the door. A freckle-faced lad in coveralls blinked and registered adolescent interest in a gap-toothed grin. He handed her the envelope. She tossed him the coin.

"Thank you, ma'am."

Oh, please not that schoolmarm address too.

He scooted down the hall.

She closed the door and slit the envelope with a finger.

Client reports bond redemptions in Rawlins and Green River.
They are following the U.P. west.

Meet me in Evanston.

— Kingsley

If nothing else the message was good for a change of scenery. Could Longstreet have known? He must have. More than likely they'd be too late for that party. The best she could hope for was pleasant diversion should Beau still be there. The thought brought a small shiver of anticipation and the hint of a smile to her lips.

Evanston

Muted late afternoon sun gave the Essex House lobby a golden glow. Cane cast a long shadow as he signed the guest register.

"Is Mr. Longstreet in?"

The clerk glanced at the pegboard where the keys were hung as if reminding himself of the guests' comings and goings. "I believe he is."

"Mind sending someone up to his room with a message?"

"Sir?"

He slid four bits across the counter. "Tell him to meet Cane in the saloon."

Fifteen minutes later Longstreet swung through the batwings. He squinted in the dim light. Cane waved from a back corner table, waiting with a bottle and two glasses.

Longstreet crossed the room and pulled back a chair.

"I take it not much turned up in Green River."

"She was there. Boatman's Bank took another bond, but I got there too late."

"I'm not surprised. I think she was here."

"You do. Why?"

"I had supper with her."

"You what?"

"I had supper with her, at least I think it was her."

"I won't ask how she got away, though that's probably the more interesting part of the story. What makes you think it was her?"

"We had the beginnings of what I thought would become a very pleasant evening until it ended rather abruptly. The next morning, she was gone."

"Did she pass a bond here?"

"No, that's the odd thing."

Cane poured drinks, knocked his back, and poured another. "Maybe not so odd. Did you tell her who you were?"

He nodded.

"You got to her before she hit the bank."

"I'm afraid so. Now she knows we're on her trail."

"They already knew."

"They?"

"She's not working alone."

"What makes you think so?"

"When was the last time a dusty rattler found its way into your second-floor hotel room?"

"Did you get bit?"

"Look at me, Beau. I'm here, ain't I?" Longstreet knocked back his drink. "Coulda been professional courtesy."

Cane poured him another. "The rattler got professional courtesy, courtesy of Forehand & Wadsworth."

"Any idea who her partner is?"

Cane shook his head. "Whoever it is must have seen me talking to the banker and put two and two together."

"So she knows who I am and somebody who plays with snakes knows who you are. Where do you suppose they are now, Ogden?"

"That would be next, but I'm guessing they will break that pattern."

"Then they could be anywhere." Longstreet swirled his drink and took a swallow. "What do you reckon we should do?"

Cane shrugged. "Wire Crook."

Shady Grove

Crook gazed at the early spring snow-capped mountainside from the veranda at the Shady Grove Rest Home and Convalescent Center. I waited patiently for him to continue.

"The news Cane and Longstreet telegraphed me from Evanston amounted to a dead end. Suddenly this didn't feel like the old days where you saddled up a good horse and went looking for the owl hoot's trail. We knew the trail sure as hell. It was a rail bed. The questions were which direction to go and how far. More importantly, how the hell do you answer those questions?"

"A good lunch, shepherd's pie as I recall, gave me a notion. I wired Salmon Chase to inquire as to any further redemption of counterfeit bonds."

His chin dropped to his chest. I waited. He snapped awake.

"Next morning, I had an answer. Rawlins and Green River were old news. At least the cashier at Salmon Chase knew we were on the case. We knew she left Evanston. We figured she wouldn't head west again. I consulted the map. Best bet was east, but you couldn't rule out going north or south overland. The first step was to notify league members to be on the lookout for an attractive woman. That should get their attention. More importantly they needed to notify their banks to be on the lookout for anyone attempting to pass Texas & Pacific bonds. Now what to tell Cane and Longstreet?"

North Platte
Nebraska

She stood at the curtained window watching thunderclouds gather in the southwestern sky beyond the rooftops across the street. She forced herself to relax. Certainly reversing her pattern would leave the big detective confused. Even if he guessed she'd gone east, he'd have no idea where. It shouldn't have come as a surprise. Escobar's abrupt order to leave Green River should have alerted her to the likelihood the authorities were on to them. Then there was Beau Longstreet. Lightning streaked out of purple green thunderheads in the distance. He was disturbing in many ways. The building trembled to a rumble of thunder she felt deep inside. Beyond the matter of legal entanglement, she'd found him disturbingly attractive. She'd seriously considered bedding him even after she knew the risk posed by his identity. Fortunately she'd overcome her sherry-mellowed judgment and avoided further complication. Lightning flashed again. Even now, she regretted it. For the first time in a long time, thunder rolled through every fiber of her being. A knock at the door recalled her from the pleasant prospect of a violent storm.

"Who is it?"

"It is I," Escobar hissed.

She opened the door to the pockmarked man with glittering ferret eyes.

"What made you come here?"

She closed the door. "The detective I met in Evanston. He's looking for us."

"He's not alone. I encountered one in Green River. That one I think will not trouble us more."

"You killed him?"

"I acquired the services of a friend to do it for us."

"Can this friend identify you?"

"*La serpiente* does not speak."

She pictured the killer in the man's eyes.

"Now tell me about this one in Evanston."

"His name is Beau Longstreet. He says he works for something called the Great Western Detective League, whatever that is."

"What does this one look like?"

Her eyes glazed at the picture. "Southern gentleman, he's big, dark, handsome."

"Seen through a woman's eyes. Did you get close to him?"

"Close, but not that close. What difference does it make?"

"Does he suspect?"

"He didn't. Then I did leave rather abruptly. He might now."

"He can identify you then."

"Yes. If he has suspicions and they are confirmed. What do we do about that?"

He drew a cigarillo out of his coat pocket, pursed thin lips, and struck a lucifer. He drew it to light and huffed out the match in a cloud of blue smoke.

"Cash a bond here. Then move on to Grand Island."

"Do you think that is wise? What if they are watching for us?"

"I, Escobar, will be at your back. If your southern gentleman detective comes for you, he will be my pleasure."

Thunder rattled the windows with the first spatters of rain.

Escobar escorted the woman to the train station in the gray light of early evening two days later. He saw her safely aboard the eastbound to Grand Island. As the train pulled slowly away from the station, his thoughts followed. *She has been exposed. She may have outlived her lovely usefulness. The Patron must be told. It is for him to decide. Pity.* He turned to the Western Union office at the depot.

CHAPTER THIRTEEN

Evanston

Samantha stepped off the train onto the platform. She took in the rough-cut depot with its official-looking sign and the suggestion of a town up the street to the north. It was a station like every other station with a town like every other one-time end-of-track town that managed to survive. The Union Pacific spawned them like saplings sprouted from the mother oak.

She glanced around the platform. No sign of Kingsley. She might find him waiting at the hotel, though more likely she'd beaten him here. She started up the boardwalk toward town. No need to ask directions. Get to the main street and look for the hotel sign. It wouldn't be far. A block north of the depot she scanned the street east and west. She found Essex House in the next block west.

The lobby too displayed a familiarity bordering on boredom, though in this case with a trace of elegance most of the others lacked. She crossed the lobby to the registration desk, enduring the gaze of an unctuous clerk with sleepy eyes, wavy hair, and a thin mustache.

"Good afternoon, madam. Welcome to Essex House. How may we be of service?"

"A room, please."

"My pleasure, madam." He spun the register and waited for her to sign.

"Very good, Miss Maples," he read. "And how long might we have the pleasure of your stay?"

His smile had the thin veneer of an undertaker.

"I'm not sure."

"Let's hope you'll grace us with your presence for some time then."

"Let's hope."

"Well, fancy meeting you here."

The familiar drawl startled her. She found a fetching smile and made a gift of it.

"Beau Longstreet, what a surprise."

"Pleasant I hope."

"Don't flatter yourself."

Flatter? The clerk reached for a key. The woman gapped the big southerner like a cat eyeing a dish of clotted cream.

130

"Room 205."

She ignored him.

"That would be your key," Longstreet said.

"Oh, yes, thank you." She nodded to the clerk.

"Here, let me help you with that valise. I'm just down the hall."

"Are you sure that's proper?"

"Do you care?"

She smiled.

He led her up the stairs.

"Where is Mr. Cane?"

"He had business with a league member at Fort Bridger. He rode out this morning. I expect him back later this evening or tomorrow sometime."

"You haven't seen Kingsley by any chance?"

"No. You're expecting him I take it."

She nodded.

"Well this is it, home sweet home room 205."

She fitted the key in the lock. "I can take that now."

He handed her the valise. "Care to have supper?"

She favored him with an interested twinkle.

"Weighing the chances of a better offer?"

She laughed, amused. "What time?"

"Shall we say six?"

"We shall."

"I'm only just down the hall, but I'll meet you in the lobby for propriety's sake."

"Ever the proper southern gentleman, I'm sure. Six, then." She let herself in and closed the door.

A delicate shade of lavender set off a flawless complexion framed in coils of blue-black curls. She floated down the stairs to the lobby, having given attentions to turning herself out for a quiet supper. Longstreet smiled to himself and let his eyes follow hers, their violet lights flashing a siren song. She'd throw him over in a heartbeat for a lead on the case, but absent such a distraction the prospects seemed rather promising. Her lavender scent coupled with an amused enigmatic smile completed the effect.

"My, my, I must say you look positively stunning, Miss Maples."

"I took a chance you'd still be here."

"You wound me. I do believe it was you who started the disappearing act."

"Woman's prerogative. Now are we going to stand here or are we going to go find a lady some supper and a libation to take the chill off?"

He offered his arm.

The café across the street was spacious by frontier standards with table linen, china, and silver. The waiter, an officious portly fellow who might have been mistaken for a schoolmaster between semesters, took their drink orders. When the drinks arrived he informed them that the special was chicken and dumplings. They ordered two.

Longstreet lifted his glass. "To Evanston."

"Which only proves we'll drink to anything." She touched her glass to his and sipped sherry.

"It's not as bad as that. I was thinking of the company."

"A glib-tongued flatterer with a mouthful of honey, now there's a man after my own heart."

"A worthy prize, I must say."

"So what sort of insight brings the dashing detective to Evanston?"

"I might ask you the same?"

"Are we talking an exchange of information?"

"Certainly, at least as far as that goes."

"Very well then. Kingsley believes they are moving west along the Union Pacific line based on the latest bond redemptions. Your turn."

"Similar thinking on our part. You'll find

out soon enough, no one has attempted to negotiate a bond at the bank here."

"Hmm, perhaps our theories are incorrect."

Longstreet furrowed his brow, weighing his thoughts.

"Or something happened to change their plan."

"Their plan?"

"All right, I probably shouldn't, but I'm going to give you this one on the house. She's not working alone."

"How do you know?"

"Cane had a run-in with someone after she left Green River. They know we are after them and they will play rough."

"What happened?"

"Someone arranged a roommate for Cane."

"A roommate?"

"A dusty rattler on the second floor of a hotel doesn't get there by accident."

"Ah!" Her hand shot to her mouth. "Is he? Is he, all right?"

"He is. I tell you that so you watch that pretty back of yours."

"Why, Beau Longstreet, if I didn't know better I might think you care."

"It's the chivalrous thing to do."

"So where does that leave us?"

The waiter arrived with two steaming plates.

"For the moment we are left with supper."

Longstreet paused in the lobby at the foot of the stairs.

"Shall I wait here?"

She tilted her chin to the side, considering under a raised brow. "Come along. Your tie is crooked."

He fingered the knotted ribbon at his throat as he followed her up the stairs. It didn't feel out of place.

She paused at the door to her room and reached for his tie. "Here, let me have a look at that." The knot pulled undone. "Oh dear, now I've made a mess of it. Here let me fix it for you."

"Don't worry about it. I'll be taking it off soon."

"I know."

She opened the door.

Gray morning light crept over the window-sill. Samantha savored the echoes to the rhythm of Longstreet's breathing. Her instincts seldom failed her where men were concerned. If anything, she'd seriously underestimated this one, delightfully so. Who could have known? She played the evening's amusements over in her mind. If a girl had to spend time in a one-horse frontier town, that's the way to do it.

The note lay on the floor at the door like a summons. Kingsley, undoubtedly he'd arrived last night. Fortunately he'd been too late to spoil the evening. What to do? Roll over and await developments? Tempting, but duty had a way of calling. She sat up. It's early. Ignore it. She slid out of bed and tiptoed across a creaky board. She picked up the note and read.

Meet me in the lobby for breakfast.

"Trouble?"

She glanced over her shoulder. Longstreet lay on his side, his head propped in one hand.

"Kingsley," she said, suddenly reminded she was naked.

"Will it wait?"

"Not for long. Why?"

"You look cold." He lifted the covers.

Magnificent. She shivered. "It'll keep that long."

Flushed and a little drowsy, Samantha found the drab tweed version of Kingsley in the lobby, tapping a polished shoe at the face of his pocket watch.

"I say, what time do you eat breakfast?"

136

"Sorry, I wasn't expecting you so early."

"Yes, well come along now, the bank opens in an hour and we shall need to be there when it does."

She followed him across the street to the café, still thinking of the more pleasant company afforded her the previous evening.

The waiter, hair slicked morning fresh, arched a brow in recognition. He showed them to a table.

"Coffee, madam?"

"Please."

"Tea if you please."

The waiter went off.

"No need to rush off to the bank," Samantha said. "She's not been here."

"How do you know?"

"Longstreet told me."

"Longstreet?"

"He and Cane are here."

"Oh? How might that have come about?"

"Same hunch as yours."

"If they've not left, they must think she might still come along."

"He didn't say."

"Of course not. Hmm," he drummed his fingers on the table as the waiter delivered steaming cups of coffee and tea.

"What will you have, madam?"

"Ham and two eggs, please."

"And you, sir?"

"Yes, that will be fine with a biscuit if you have one."

"Fresh and warm, thank you, sir."

Kingsley followed him with a vacant stare. "She might also have passed Evanston in favor of Ogden."

"If your theory holds, that is definitely a possibility."

"Perhaps we should pursue that possibility."

"Why don't you cover Ogden, while I keep an eye on Longstreet and Cane." She hoped the suggestion sounded convincingly professional.

"An eye on Longstreet, is it? Yes I suppose you are likely to get more out of him than I."

The visitor bell clanged. Kingsley glanced at the sun-splashed doorway. "Speak of the devil, here they come now. Cane, Longstreet, top of the morning," he waved.

"Kingsley, Miss Maples," Cane said.

"Might you gentlemen care to join us?"

"Sorry, we've business to discuss. Perhaps another time."

"Ah, business. Any information we might exchange?"

Longstreet chuckled.

"Did I say something amusing?"

"You forget, Sir Reggie, I've been on your side of one of those information exchanges."

"Fiddlesticks. You're certainly not going to hold that Sam Bass gambit against me are you? I'm totally reformed and scrupulously honest in my dealings."

"I'm pleased to hear that." He turned to the waiter. "If you don't mind we'll take that table in the far corner."

"As you wish, sir."

Kingsley watched them go. "I suppose I deserved that."

"What happened with Sam Bass?"

"Simple misunderstanding, nothing more, it just happened to work in our favor. I suppose it is best if you stay here. I'll catch the noon train to Ogden."

CHAPTER FOURTEEN

Grand Island

Grand Island grew up on the banks of the Platte River, a branch of which circled the town several miles to the north, giving early French explorers the illusion of a great island. In more recent times the town sprawled south of the Union Pacific tracks in a hash-work of clapboard and brick structures with edifice architectures reflecting the population's German ethnic roots. Walking Front Street from the depot to the hotel, Cecile overheard locals conversing in German as often as in English.

The Grand Hotel, with its elaborate façade, massive polished lobby, and oversized velvet-covered furnishings, reeked of elegance and security that might have been the envy of most frontier banks. She found the note from Escobar under her door two days after her arrival. The note provided the address of a house where he was staying. *A house, not the hotel, that's odd. Why?*

Why soon became apparent. The *house* offered more than simple lodging. The *house* might more properly be called a bordello. She found it amusing. The pockmarked little weasel paid for his pleasure. A somewhat bored hostess in a revealing gown showed her to a room and disappeared down the hall. Being unfamiliar with the etiquette in such establishments she knocked on the door.

"It's open."

She opened the door. Escobar lay on a rumpled bed smoking a thin cigar. The room was small and sparsely furnished. Stale air smelled male with a residue of cheap perfume.

"I hope I'm not interrupting anything."

"I'm relaxing. You didn't have any trouble finding the place."

"No, though, I must say I got a rather reproving reaction from the desk clerk when I asked directions. I now understand why. Not exactly the Grand Hotel. It must be less expensive."

"It costs more. The hotel would be the obvious place for your detective friend to look for us. This is safer."

"Safer for you, what am I, a bit of cheese to bait a trap?"

"They have no way of knowing where we are. You haven't seen any sign of them I'm sure."

"So much for defending your choice of . . . accommodations for reasons of security. No I haven't seen them and I have no plans to do so, either. It's time to head west and let things cool off."

"Not yet. I'm awaiting instructions from my superior."

"Did you cash the North Platte letter?"

He nodded around a puff of cigar smoke.

"They'll know where we are soon enough."

"Sí, and they will look for us here."

"My point exactly, it is time to move west."

He shook his head. "There is time to pass one more bond in Omaha. Then you may go to San Francisco. I will meet you there, when I finish here."

"Finish what?"

"You are right about your detective friend coming here after North Platte. You will not be here. I will be waiting, with a surprise to slow down these pursuers."

Ogden
Utah Territory
Kingsley paused on the sun-soaked board-

walk outside the First Bank of Ogden. He checked his watch. Nine thirty, thirty minutes after the bank opened. The cashier's reaction to his inquiry as to Texas & Pacific bearer bonds surprised him. It seems the local sheriff alerted the banker to be on the lookout for the bogus bonds. It smacked of Crook's detective league. Nothing remained for the rest of the day but to wait. Wait for what? He had a nagging feeling he'd gotten his hunch too late. The woman was either uncommonly good or uncommonly lucky. He snapped his watch closed and strolled down the block toward the Western Union office at the depot. He'd check in with Chicago on the chance they might have a further report on his query.

The depot stood on the north bank of the Weber River with the town grown up to the north. He sent his wire off to the head office and returned to his hotel. He hoped he'd not have to spend much time in this dreadfully decent town with a strict Mormon abhorrence for vice. He saw no sign of whiskey or gambling or . . . whiskey or gambling.

Evanston

It was her assignment after all. Samantha took up her position on a settee across from

143

the registration desk as late afternoon sun turned the lobby a golden glow. She busied herself with the daily edition of the *Evanston Free Tribune,* giving plausible excuse to a vigil for Longstreet or Cane. To be honest Cane was incidental to her interest. Her mind wandered over the news pages, her thoughts more taken with the big southerner. Sooner or later she reasoned he'd pass this way to supper.

Within the hour footfalls on the stairs descending from above rewarded her patience. Longstreet came down the stairs accompanied by Cane. She pretended not to notice.

"Good evening, Sam."

His eyes smiled somewhat more than in greeting.

"Sam?" Cane said.

"Social ruffle," Longstreet said. "Waiting for Sir Reggie?"

"He's moved on to more pressing matters," she said.

"I see. Briscoe and I were about to go out for a bite of supper. Care to join us?"

"That's a far better prospect than dining alone, as long as Mr. Cane doesn't mind."

Cane looked from one to the other. "Mind? I might be the one intruding. Please come along if you're not put off by hickory

144

and leather."

"Come now, you're far more charming than that." She took an arm from each as they turned out the door.

"Hear that, Beau? It's charming I am. Who knew?"

"Your secret's safe with me, old man."

"Old man, why you pup."

"Boys, please, no fighting before supper, it'll sour your digestion."

The waiter seated the three of them with a still more curious look.

"Let me see, sherry for the lady, a whiskey for you, sir."

"I'll have a beer," Cane said.

The waiter scurried off.

"So, Sir Reggie is off to more pressing business, what's up?"

Samantha cocked an amused eye at Longstreet. "Are we talking an information exchange?"

He laughed. "No, just fishing."

"At least you're honest. Kingsley says you had some sort of a misunderstanding over an information exchange in regard to Sam Bass. What happened?"

Cane shook his head. "No misunderstanding to it. We were both chasing Bass. He got away from us in Nebraska at Buffalo Station. We agreed to exchange information. I gave up mine. Kingsley gave me some. It was true enough, he just chose to leave out a rather important detail. That was when Beau here was still workin' for Pinkerton."

"Reggie didn't feel the need of an honest and complete exchange. The part he left out made the exchange rather meaningless for our part."

The waiter arrived with the drinks.

"The special this evening is chicken fried steak and potatoes."

They nodded all around.

"You mean Kingsley didn't play fair?"

"Nope." He lifted his chin to Longstreet. "Beau here filled in the blanks behind his back. That's when I first started thinking he might be a better partner than competitor."

She smiled with a twinkle in her eye. "So you really are honest."

He lifted his glass. "Guilty as charged, ma'am."

Supper passed to apple pie and coffee.

The waiter appeared to clear the dessert plates.

"Will there be anything else this evening?"

Longstreet deferred to Samantha.

"I might have a sherry nightcap."

"Make it two."

Cane yawned. "I'll leave you two to that. My night is already capped." He pushed back his chair and nodded to Samantha. "Beau, I'll see you in the morning."

"Good night, Briscoe."

The visitor bell bid adieu as the sherry arrived.

"So, Kingsley's other business didn't include you."

"Are we fishing again?" She lifted her glass.

"Just curious."

"A girl might hope for more. Actually I volunteered to stay behind to keep an eye on you."

"Does that make me a suspect?"

"Yesterday you were a suspect. Today you're guilty as charged."

"Have I been sentenced yet?"

"One more of these and I believe that can be arranged."

"Waiter!"

Ogden

He'd no more than raised an adequate lather when the knock sounded at the door.

"Telegram for Mr. Kingsley."

He set down his shaving mug and fished in his trouser pocket for a quarter. He tossed the coin to the messenger in exchange for the envelope. He tore it open.

Client reports fifth bond redeemed in North Platte.

— Pinkerton

There it is. Just as he suspected, she'd broken her pattern. He returned to the mirror over the dresser and wet his razor in the basin. Smooth, clean razor strokes lubricated some of his best thinking. She'd be long gone from North Platte. That was old news. He rinsed the razor in the basin. The question was, where next? The Union Pacific route map played through his mind. Stroke, rinse, stroke, Grand Island, that was it. He'd wire Maples with instructions to embark thitherward with alacrity. He'd toddle along to tidy up in North Platte. He wiped the residue of his shave on a towel.

Evanston

Pity, Samantha crumpled the telegram. Duty calls. She debated a caring farewell to Beau. Too complicated, he'd want to know where she was going and why. Business, she decided, is business. A simple note would suffice. She smiled, confident she could manage forgiveness later.

■ ■ ■ ■

Duty calls,

— Sam

Longstreet shook his head.

"Something the matter, sir?"

The desk clerk who'd given him the note from Samantha had likely noticed their comings and goings.

"Miss Maples didn't by any chance say where she was going, did she?"

"No, sir. I'm afraid not."

"That from Crook?" Cane swung around the stairway turn post and tilted his chin at the note.

"No. Samantha, she's left."

"What and no forwarding address?"

"How did you guess?"

"I'm a detective."

"Now what?"

"You'll get a good night's rest?"

"Very funny."

"We wire Crook. Something must have happened, another bond maybe."

Shady Grove

"Cane's telegram proved timely."

We were seated on the veranda enjoying an unseasonably warm May afternoon. The

149

mountain peaks in the distance remained snow-capped to be sure, but sun soaked the wide spacious veranda that ran all along the back of the Shady Grove Rest Home and Convalescent Center. Penny set our place at the far end of the porch where our conversation wouldn't disturb the napping of other residents enjoying such a pleasant breath of spring.

"Timely, how so?"

"Later that very day North Platte Sheriff Matt David reported their bank had been notified that a bond they'd taken as collateral had been found to be counterfeit. He wondered if that might have anything to do with the alert I'd sent out. He wondered, can you imagine?"

"Not I. Information, I guess, doesn't always inform."

"The banker who suffered a preventable loss of one hundred thousand dollars might have considered it malfeasance in office. At least that cleared up the matter of a proper instruction for Cane and Longstreet."

"So you sent them to North Platte."

"Heavens no. I sent them to Grand Island."

"Grand Island? But the bank was in North Platte."

"We weren't interested in the last bank to

fall victim. We were interested in the next bank."

"Time for lunch, Colonel."

My Penny rescued me from mortal embarrassment. She looked bright and lovely as a spring wild flower. Spring, it surely did turn a young man's thoughts to fancy.

"Lunch, by that you mean yet another tasteless assault on a palate once accustomed to better fare."

"Oh, come now, Colonel, it's not as bad as all that. If it weren't for your complaints of the food, you'd have no complaint with the world."

"You say. Food is only the beginning of my complaints. The 'world' as you phrase it, has no concern for the plight of an old man incarcerated to rest. And what have you two planned for this afternoon?"

"A picnic, that is if Penny cares to join me."

"If she cares. Robert the girl is dumbstruck with you, though I can't for the life of me figure out why."

She blushed. I liked it.

"You are getting old when you can no longer remember what it's like to be young."

"Hmm, yes I suppose that could be it. Well just remember which side of your toast is buttered in the matter of these stories." He patted the whiskey bottle under his lap robe with a wink. "See you next week, Robert. Now take me away, fair Penny, lest I further delay young romance in season."

She blushed again.

Chapter Fifteen

Grand Island

Patron favored the De Chico brothers when the work became messy. They stepped off the train from Cheyenne and proceeded across the tracks from the depot to the Red Garter Saloon on the other side of town. The brothers took a back corner table with a bottle of tequila. Ramon, the leader, told the bartender to notify Escobar of their arrival. He sent a young boy in bib overalls off on the errand while Ramon joined his brothers.

The older and younger De Chicos followed the lead of their middle brother. It wasn't because of his size. The older brother, Louis, was a bull of a man, strong and powerful. He was also dull-witted. He seldom said more than a grunt, whether expressing consent or uncertainty. Ramon didn't lead because of his skill with weapons. That distinction went to younger

153

brother, Raul, who turned cat-quick and deadly with both his gun and a knife. Ramon led because the other brothers knew he was bright.

Thirty minutes later, Escobar entered the dingy saloon. He cut his eyes across the bar, ignoring the hopeful come-hither of a hard-worn whore, drawn as if by instinct to the back corner. He crossed the room and took the fourth chair.

"Ramon," he said, exchanging nods with the other two.

"Señor Escobar, you have work for us?"

"Sí." He poured tequila and swilled fiery agave. "You have no lime or salt?"

"Gringo cantina what do you expect? Now, how then may we be of service?"

"We wish to eliminate a problem."

"How many are this problem?"

"One that I know of, though there could be more by now."

"And where do we find this problem?"

"At the bank."

"You wish us to rob it?"

He shook his head as he poured another drink.

"The problem we wish to eliminate is a detective who is following one of my associates. Mi Patron will be very grateful if this detective gives up his search, *permanente-*

mente."

"*Bueno.* Where is this bank?"

"In town, I will show you."

"And how will we know this detective?"

"I will wait nearby and give you the sign."

The gold painted sign in the window glinted late afternoon sun. It proclaimed Farmer's and Merchant's Bank of Grand Island. *Very impressive,* Samantha thought as she entered the lobby. The tap of her heels on the polished wood floor drew the attention of the teller at the nearest cage.

"May I help you?"

"Where might I find the cashier?"

"Mr. Bixby." She pointed to a dark-suited gentleman seated at a desk beyond the far end of the teller counter.

She crossed the lobby to the low railing separating the important banker from the bank's run-of-the-mill customer.

"Mr. Bixby?"

He glanced over the wire rim of his spectacles. His brown barbered hair was a little gray at the temples; his stern brown eyes softened at the prospect.

"Alexander Bixby," he rose. "How may I be of service?"

"Samantha Maples, Pinkerton Agency, I'd like a word with you if I might."

He opened a gate in the low railing inviting her to approach his desk.

"Pinkerton, I must say you're nothing like any other Pinkerton Agent I've ever encountered."

"Women agents often have that effect on unsuspecting men. It disarms them. That's why Mr. Pinkerton employs them."

"I never knew. Please have a seat and let me assure you, I'm unarmed."

She smiled. "I am," and took the offered chair.

He took his seat.

"Now what can I do for you?"

"I am investigating a forgery ring engaged in passing Texas & Pacific bonds."

"In rather large denominations."

"Why, yes, how do you know?"

"Regrettably Miss Maples, you and the sheriff are both too late."

"Then they've been here."

"I'm afraid so."

"An attractive woman used the bond to secure a letter of credit."

He nodded.

"Did she say anything that might give a clue to her whereabouts?"

"One could scarcely rely on anything that woman might say, but no, she didn't."

"I'm sorry for your loss, Mr. Bixby."

"I haven't lost anything, yet."

"You will."

His countenance sank crestfallen and sour.

"One more thing, you mentioned the sheriff being late too."

"He tried to warn me. He had a bulletin he called it, from some association he belongs to. Missed her by two days."

"Thank you for your time, Mr. Bixby."

"You will let me know if you apprehend this woman."

"Of course. Good day."

Leaving the bank a metallic flash of sunlight across the street caught her eye. A large dark-skinned man seated in front of a cigar store covered something with his coat. A gun? She glanced to her left, preparing to cross the street to a millinery shop. Another dark-skinned man lounged against the corner of a building in the next block. Was he Indian? Mexican, possibly? She crossed the street to admire a bonnet in the shop window. The window reflection revealed yet another dark-skinned man, two doors up from the bank. It struck her as too odd to credit coincidence. The sheriff's warning likely meant Longstreet was on his way here. She remembered Cane's encounter with the snake in his hotel room. This smelled like a trap.

Omaha

Nebraska First Bank Cashier Orville Mather folded thick fingers across the vest warming his paunch. *Who would ever take such a refined and beautiful woman for a common criminal? Well, not really all that common. Common criminals didn't typically go in for one-hundred-thousand-dollar forgery swindles; and good ones too by the look of this one. No, this was definitely an uncommon criminal, though criminal nonetheless. Had it not been for Sheriff Bassett's timely warning he might have been taken in.* He stroked his mustache in his most thoughtful banker demeanor.

"The bank will be most happy to accommodate your transaction, Miss Reed, though I'm afraid given the amount, we shall have to redeem the bond before issuing the bank's letter of credit. It shouldn't take more than a week's time. We can deposit the proceeds into an account you may draw on, or we can wire our letter to you or your designate at your instruction."

"But, Mr. Mather, I haven't got a week's time. That's why I need the letter now. Good heavens, this is a Texas & Pacific bond. It couldn't be any more secure if it were certified by the U.S. Mint."

"I understand that, Miss Reed; but I don't

158

make the bank's policy, I simply enforce it."

"Isn't there something you can do for me?"

Her lashes fluttered in appeal.

The woman is good, very good.

"Sorry, I'm afraid the matter is out of my hands."

"Very well then, my bond if you please." She extended a gloved hand. "I shall simply have to take my business elsewhere."

He handed over the bond. She tucked it in her purse and left with little more than a curt nod. She did leave a little more behind as Mather watched her leave.

"Mr. Sullivan."

The senior teller left his cage.

"Sir?"

"Go along to the sheriff's office and tell Sheriff Bassett I need to see him at once."

"Yes, sir."

Shady Grove

"So you got her in Omaha. What happened to Longstreet and Cane in Grand Island?"

The colonel shook his head. "Not so fast, Robert. We didn't get her in Omaha. Tony Bassett, Omaha sheriff at the time, got word the woman had attempted to cash a bond at the Nebraska First Bank. He thought she might next try the Bank of Omaha. He informed me he intended to set up a watch for her there. I determined Longstreet and Cane should join him and dispatched a wire forthwith. Unfortunately, my communiqué found them variously occupied by more pressing matters."

"Speaking of pressing matters, Colonel, lunch is served."

My lovely Penny interrupted.

He shook his white mane with a wince. "Robert, I would be cautious were I you when it comes to this woman's standards where food is concerned. The tasteless fare they masquerade before us here as food scarcely meets the test of veracity."

"You don't appear to be wasting away."

"He's not, Robert. 'Tiz only he's incorrigible peevishness running away with himself again."

"Incorrigible? Peevish? Hardly, my dear. Jaded perhaps, but you wouldn't understand. You don't have to eat the gruel. I am fairly wasting away inside. And my taste buds? I'd venture to say they haven't been used since the day I arrived."

CHAPTER SIXTEEN

Grand Island

A long whistle blast followed by two shorts announced their arrival. Cane nudged Longstreet awake. Dull gray light seeped through the dust-streaked window as the train slow-rolled into the depot. A knot of departing passengers waited on the station platform. The car lurched to a steam hiss and the squeal of metallic brakes. Cane slid into the aisle and tugged his valise out of the overhead rack. Longstreet stretched and yawned.

"Come along, Sleeping Beauty, time to get back to work."

Longstreet hauled himself out of the window seat, grabbed his bag, and followed Cane up the aisle to the coach entry. A warm dry wind beneath a thick deck of cloud greeted the arriving passengers. Longstreet followed Cane woodenly, not fully awake.

"Beau."

A familiar female voice brought him up short. He seldom forgot one he remembered on those terms. He turned and smiled.

"Samantha, what a pleasant surprise. I'd ask what you are doing here, but what would be the point of that?"

Cane heard the exchange and returned through the arriving and departing crosscurrent.

"I'm here, though the surprise may not be all that pleasant."

"Is it something I said?"

"Don't be silly." She patted his cheek, then caught herself, conscious of Cane. "Remember your friend, the one who plays with snakes?"

Cane lifted a brow.

"I think he's here with three or four new friends, two-legged this time. I spotted them watching the bank."

"What makes you think they're watching for us?" Cane asked.

"Call it women's intuition, that and too much to credit coincidence."

He exchanged a glance with Longstreet. "Then I expect it's best if we don't just drop in on the bank."

"That's why I'm here. I think we may find opportunity in this."

"How so?" Longstreet felt the need to seem relevant to the conversation.

"These, ah, gentlemen are looking for you. They don't know we know they are laying in wait. You two go to the Paradise Hotel and lay low. I'll fetch the sheriff and together we can arrange a surprise for your new friends."

"Ever the clever girl." Longstreet held her gaze. "Paradise Hotel, is it?"

"It's not what you think. Let's just say it's unlikely you'll be discovered there."

Unlikely indeed, the Paradise proved to be a second-class hotel in a town with two classes, first and last. Not surprisingly they had rooms. Somewhat more surprising they passed an old oaken scrub bucket and mop idling in the uncarpeted hallway leading to those rooms.

Thirty minutes later Samantha arrived with a cherry cheeked, portly, bespectacled man wearing a derby hat and frock coat.

"Chauncy Tubbs, sheriff." He extended his hand.

"Briscoe Cane, Great Western Detective League, this is my partner Beau Longstreet."

Hands shook. "A couple of Colonel Crook's boys, eh? I'm a league member myself. I'm surprised you're working with Pinkerton."

"She's saving my life," Longstreet said.

"Lucky for me," Cane said.

The sheriff glanced around the dingy lobby. "Is there somewhere we can talk?"

"My room," Longstreet said. "There's not much charm and even less to sit on, but it's cozy." He took Samantha's arm and led the way upstairs.

The room offered a bed, dresser, spindle-back chair, and privacy.

"Miss Maples and I took a stroll by the bank on our way over here. As she says there appear to be three men, half-breed, maybe Mexican, on watch near the bank. Does that mean anything to either of you?"

Cane shrugged. "We're investigating a forgery ring passing Texas & Pacific bonds."

"I only recently received a dodger on that from the colonel. I tried to warn Alex Bixby over at the bank, but unfortunately I got there too late."

"Well that's been the story of this case," Cane continued. "We've been a step or two behind these people every step of the way. They know we're coming, though. Someone dropped a dusty gray rattler off in my room in Green River."

"Dusty gray's ain't all that common. I'm

surprised you're still here."

"Lucky shot."

"For a fact."

"I'm impressed once again," Samantha said. "Sheriff, how do you propose we arrange this little fandango?"

"Well, as it stands, unless you've got some specific charge to make, I couldn't arrest 'em for much more than suspicion of loitering."

"We'll have to smoke 'em out," Cane said.

"How do you propose to do that?"

"I go to the bank."

"Bait the trap, you mean," Tubbs said.

Longstreet held up a hand. "He means we go to the bank."

"I'm the one they know, Beau."

"You think they aren't on the lookout for me after Evanston?"

"What happened in Evanston?" Samantha asked.

"Long story."

"I'm sure it is."

"Briscoe, if you're gonna play cheese to the rats, I'm going with you. Someone's got to look after your back."

"Who's going to look after your back?"

"The sheriff here, right, Sheriff?"

"I've just got but one deputy." He tilted his hat back and dabbed perspiration on a shiny bald pate. "Sorry, kind of stuffy in here."

"Cozy," Longstreet said.

"You'll need a couple more. Can you get them by the time the bank opens in the morning?" Cane asked.

Tubbs nodded. "I don't like the idea of shootin' up my main street in broad daylight. You two show up, those gents likely make it a gun play."

"That's where you and your deputies come in," Cane said. "You cover 'em so you can step in if they try to make a play. Can you do that?"

"It's still risky."

"It is. Then again if me and Beau here walk into that bank, your main street's likely to get shot up either way. If we outnumber 'em and hit 'em by surprise, the party could be over before any real damage gets done."

Tubbs nodded. "All right."

Samantha bunched her fists on her hips. "What about me?"

Longstreet smiled. "Your job is to be on the lookout for the woman."

"You mean the woman from Evanston?"

A breath from the icehouse cooled Longstreet's brow.

Paradise. Longstreet hung his coat on a

spindle-back chair with a wobbly leg. He removed his shoulder rig and set the Colt pocket pistol on the scarred dresser. He peeled off his shirt and hung it over his coat. He opened the cracked window in hope of catching an evening breeze. The tattered calico curtains furled fresh air into the stuffy room. It cooled the dampness against his chest. A soft knock sounded at the door. Not much like Cane to come calling this time of night. He glanced at his gun, eased it out of the holster, and crossed the small room to the door. He listened. Nothing. He flattened along the wall beside the door frame, raised the pistol, grasped the knob, and jerked the door open.

"Don't shoot," she whispered with a throaty laugh.

"What brings you by at this hour?"

"A line of questioning I'm not satisfied with. May I come in?"

She stepped inside without waiting for an answer and closed the door with a soft click. "You can put that gun away. I assure you I mean you no harm."

He put the pistol on the dresser and drew her close. Reflected lamplight flickered in violet eyes. He held them. "Now what is this pressing line of questioning you've not satisfied?"

"Oh, I think you know."

He shrugged.

"Evanston."

"Not much to tell."

"This afternoon you said it was a long story."

"I exaggerated."

"I don't believe you. Now out with it, the truth, the whole truth and nothing but the truth."

"Nothing but the truth?"

"We'll see about that. The truth first."

"You smell like lilacs."

"What does that have to do with Evanston?"

"It's the truth."

"You're incorrigible."

"At least I'm honest."

"That remains to be seen." She placed her fingers against his chest and gently pushed him back to sit on the bed. "Now out with it."

"I think I saw her."

"You think you saw her. What makes you think so?"

"We had supper."

"You had supper."

"We did."

"And from that, you think this mystery woman is our perpetrator? That seems a rather ambitious conclusion. What makes you think so?"

"She disappeared rather abruptly after finding out what I was doing in Evanston."

"And this abrupt disappearance, did it occur the next morning?"

"I don't know."

"You don't know. What did you do after supper?"

"We parted company."

"Abruptly?"

"Quite. Why is that so important?"

"Just curious."

"Just curious." He rose and drew her closer. "I think you're jealous."

"Don't flatter yourself."

"I promised you nothing but the truth."

"And you believe you've fulfilled that promise?"

"Yes. Now I have an unsatisfied question." He took her in his arms. "Why did you tip us off to the trap?"

She patted his cheek and glanced down. "What, and waste all that while you get yourself killed?"

"Waste not, want not."

The bank opened at nine o'clock the following morning. Cane and Longstreet started south on the boardwalk fronting the

Paradise Hotel buffeted by a strong warm and dry west wind. Cane noticed the spring in his partner's step.

"Don't you ever get tired?"

"Tired? Me? Oh that. Sure, but I take a little snooze and next thing you know I'm good as new."

Cane shook his head. They rounded the corner on the north side of Fourth Street and turned northeast following the run of the U.P. tracks across the street. Bootheels tapped a gallows hollow roll. Cane squinted into bright morning sun. Up the block, beyond the bank a dark figure crossed the street and paused at a shop window.

"The deck's cut. They're ready to deal."

"What makes you think so?"

"Up the street, a man just crossed to this side."

"People cross streets all the time."

"Not this time. He's the lookout tellin' the others we're comin' this way."

Longstreet reached inside his coat, drew his Colt, and dropped his hand to his side.

Standing in the doorway to a millinery shop, Ramon relayed Louis's signal to Raul in the alley across the street. He listened for the footfalls that would foretell their approach. Louis would be ambling down the street toward the bank. They would have them, three against two in a cross fire. It would be over in seconds and they would be gone. Escobar and his patron would be pleased.

Cane stepped off the boardwalk to the mouth of an alley, separating the elaborate front of a music hall from a tobacconist and a millinery shop. He glanced down the alley, making eye contact with one of Tubbs's men who tossed his head up the street. They were getting close.

"Won't be long now," he said, unlimbering the .44 at his hip.

They passed the tobacco shop. Cane sensed the shadowy presence as they passed the next doorway. He felt for the blade sheathed behind the holstered .44. He counted his steps . . . two, three, four, movement. He spun into a crouch facing the man who stepped out of the doorway with a gun.

"Drop it!" Tubbs's deputy ordered from the mouth of the alley.

The man turned, gun in hand.

Cane threw. The blade struck the assailant in back of the right shoulder, ruining the assassin's aim. The shot exploded harmlessly over the deputy's head. Longstreet grabbed the wounded gunman and disarmed him.

Across the street Sheriff Tubbs stepped out of an alley, holding a second man at the point of a sawed-off shotgun. Up the street, two more deputies had a big man in cuffs. Tubbs crossed the street with his prisoner.

"Sorry about the gunfire, Sheriff."

"One shot, three killers in custody, and no harm done. I reckon the good people of Grand Island got what they pay law enforcement for."

The sheriff's men were waiting for them. The gringos must have known, but how? Escobar ground his teeth. The Di Chico brothers were professionals. They would not willingly expose him. They knew the Don's influence reached even into the prisons for those who might betray him. Still, with these law dogs on the prowl, it would be best to catch the next train to Omaha. Perhaps the woman would have more success there.

CHAPTER SEVENTEEN

Shady Grove

I arrived the following Saturday morning still fairly flummoxed from the prior evening's sparking on the porch swing at Penny's rooming house. We'd gone out for our usual Friday night supper and ended the evening enjoying each other's company and the symphony of a summer night. In truth as things progress between us, the symphony was more accompaniment to enjoying each other. I hadn't slept very well. Clearly our love needed something more permanent than a porch swing. I owed my wakefulness to that admission along with some physical agitation that brought me to it. Indeed we were truly in love. But what was to be done about it? I could scarcely entertain proposing marriage on the meager wages of a cub reporter at a small western daily. In the end, I'd stolen a few moments' rest, pinning my hopes on the publisher's acceptance of my book submission.

With all that on the mind it's little wonder I'd forgotten it. The thought never crossed my mind until Penny left the colonel and me to our weekly visit on the veranda. He offered the empty bottle for the presumed return of a full one. I accepted the empty and steeled it away. His hand remained extended expectantly.

"Well?"

"I'm afraid I've forgotten."

"You've forgotten."

"I apologize. I've had a lot on my mind of late."

"I'm sure you have. I don't know which one of you is the worse for it. But what of me? Am I to suffer slings and arrows for the twining of your heartstrings?"

"It has nothing to do with . . ."

"Oh please. I'm old not addled. Fortunately for both of us, I have an alternate plan."

I listened.

"My room is on the ground floor, north-west corner in the rear. I shall be at my window at nightfall. You should have no trouble finding it. You can deliver my weekly stipend there with no one the wiser."

"Are you suggesting I sneak onto the grounds in the dead of night like a thief?"

"Of course not. You're not about to steal anything and nightfall is hardly the dead of night. Think of it as an *unannounced visit.* You'll merely be bringing comfort to an old soldier for the good of your book, don't you see."

"But what if I'm caught? What if Penny finds out? We're to go to the moving picture show this evening. If I'm here, I could be late."

"Robert, you're a resourceful young fellow. Who would ever think to pin a courtship on a porch swing? I have every confidence you will work out our little arrangement."

Porch swing! How could he possibly know about that? Curious as I might be, I dared not ask.

"I'll be along."

"There's a good lad. Now where were we?"

I consulted my notes. *What would I tell Penny?*

"Cane and Longstreet had managed to foil the ambush at the bank in Grand Island."

"That's right. My telegram dispatching them to Omaha arrived at the conclusion of that episode."

Omaha

Escobar sat on a bench in a back corner of the depot smoking a cigarillo behind a newspaper. The distant sound of the eastbound train whistle told him he had another two hours to wait for his westbound connection. Had he known, he wouldn't have bothered to come to Omaha in the first place. A note and a telegram greeted him at the hotel registration desk. The note was from the woman. Her attempt at cashing a bond ran into difficulty. The banker insisted on redeeming the bond before issuing a letter of credit. She rightly suspected a trap and left word he should meet her in San Francisco. She could think on her feet. The telegram from Don Victor, sent through his intermediary, instructed him to leave the Union Pacific line and relocate operations south along the Texas & Pacific, a move that should put enough distance between them and their pursuers to allow them to complete the client contract. Don Victor was El Anillo Patron for a reason.

Outside beyond the platform the engine coughed to the shriek of brakes and whistle. Escobar glanced out a streaked window behind his paper, watching the river of humanity disembark from the train. Something told him his vigilance would be rewarded. It was. The big one made the pair of detectives stand out in the crowd. He shook his head. They should have died in Grand Island. Each man carried a small traveling bag. They crossed the platform and disappeared from sight headed for town. They would find nothing. He would be long gone before the detectives realized they'd lost the trail yet again. Still they had too much good fortune. The crooked one had escaped him twice now. That man owed him a debt that must be collected before it became a stain on his professional reputation. Before this ended he would collect from both of them.

He folded the paper, reminded he must wire the Don. The Di Chico brothers were loyal soldados. The Don would wish they should have adequate legal representation. They would soon be released for lack of evidence.

Escobar did not notice the last passenger to exit the last car. A raven-haired beauty in widow's weeds she wore a feathered hat and lace veil concealing her features. She followed the two detectives up the street at a distance.

Sheriff Tony Bassett was a long-legged country boy with half-lidded eyes, a droopy mustache, rumpled appearance, and unruffled demeanor.

"Colonel wired you'd be along." He shook hands with Longstreet and Cane. "Glad to have the two of you here. We don't get much call on counterfeit bonds in these parts. Hell, I'm not sure I'd know one if it was to bite me."

"That's the sinister beauty of them bonds," Cane said. "You don't feel the bite until you try to redeem one. By then you got a bad case of their poison."

"So far we done pretty good on that score here. I informed my banks directly after receiving the colonel's dodger, we ain't got but two in town. Sure enough she showed up at Nebraska First. Orville Mather, he's the cashier over there, he talked to her real nice. Tried to stall her by takin' a few days to collect the thing before he was to cash it. She got a little skittery, took her bond, and left. Mr. Mather notified me right off. I figured she might try Bank of Omaha next. I got a deputy watchin' the bank."

"It sounds like you've done all the right things, Sheriff," Longstreet said.

"It surely has worked out for the best so far."

"It will, once we capture the woman and whoever she's workin' with."

"That would be icing on the cake. Either way them bankers is grateful for me savin' 'em from what coulda been a passel of trouble. Grateful bankers is a good thing when a sheriff is runnin' for reelection."

Longstreet caught Cane's eye with a half smile. "All right, Sheriff Bassett, let's go meet these grateful bankers of yours."

"Please call me Tony. Where'd you like to start?"

"The one you have under surveillance, Bank of Omaha. You can call me Beau and this cantankerous character here is Briscoe."

Notions they called it. Mostly it consisted of sewing things. About all Samantha knew of such things was which end of the needle you shouldn't poke yourself with. Being a woman, she attracted no attention pretending to examine the merchandise at the front of the store with a good view of the sheriff's office across the street. Longstreet and Cane had gone there from the depot. Likely this was the source of the information that brought them to Omaha. It wasn't long before they reemerged with a gangly gaited companion she took for the sheriff. The sheriff led them up the street. She watched them, replacing a spool of thread in the display case. Between the sheriff's gait and

Cane's awkward frame they made a sight reminiscent of a broken-down swayback horse. She chuckled. A trio sure to strike mortal fear in the heart of any self-respecting desperado. She left the store and followed them up the street, keeping a discreet distance.

They crossed into the next block and paused in front of a building on the corner. The sign read Bank of Omaha. The sheriff nodded across the street with a wave to a man seated on a bench in front of a cigar store. If they're watching the bank, they expected something. She'd seen enough. Time to check into the hotel and wire developments to Kingsley.

Bassett led the way across the lobby to a large polished desk in the back corner. The desk provided an imposing barrier to protect a mousy little man with a starched collar.

"Afternoon, Wilford."

"Afternoon, Sheriff. Does this visit suggest we have something afoot on the bond fraud?"

"I wanted to introduce you to these two gents. They're investigating the counterfeit ring we're on the lookout for."

"Briscoe Cane." He offered his hand across the desk.

"Wilford Pendergast, Cashier." He returned a birdlike shake.

"Beau Longstreet, Mr. Pendergast."

"Briscoe and Beau are with the Great Western Detective League I told you about."

"Pleasure to meet both of you. The bank is indebted to you for the timely warning the sheriff was able to offer us in regard to these nefarious characters. I understand others have not been so fortunate."

"I'm afraid not, Mr. Pendergast. Glad we could help," Cane said.

"I take it all's quiet," Bassett said. The banker nodded. "Just as well. I thought you should know who Briscoe and Beau are as you will likely see them in the course of our surveillance."

"We're pleased to have all the protection the law can afford."

"If either of you need anything, we'll be staying at the hotel," Cane said.

"We'll check in in the morning."

Longstreet noticed it on entering the hotel lobby, something fresh to go with the usual scent of musty fabric and wood polish. The clerk spun the register. Cane signed. Longstreet placed it as he scratched his signature.

"I'd like to leave a message for Miss Maples."

Cane arched a brow.

"We don't have anyone registered by that name," the clerk said.

"I see that. She's medium height, dark hair, quite pretty."

"That could be Mrs. McGarritty."

The name immediately above Cane's on the register. "I'm sure it is."

The clerk handed over a note paper and pencil. Longstreet scrawled.

"Supper?" Cane asked.

He nodded. "Will you be joining us?"

"I believe I'll have a tray sent to my room. I'm behind on my scripture reading. You might do well to consider some of that for yourself."

Longstreet handed the note to the clerk. "He can be such a curmudgeon."

She descended the stairs to the lobby promptly at six thirty. Longstreet smiled.

"Punctuality, a rare character in beautiful women."

"I'm sure you have vast experience in that regard, Mr. Longstreet."

"Please, Beau."

"Dare I dream? How did you know I was here?"

"Lilacs."

"Lilacs?"

"The lobby smelled of lilacs."

"I shall have to be more discreet in my use of perfume. I could have been found by some unscrupulous charlatan."

"Reserve judgment on that until you see what you've caught."

She smiled a mixture of mystic and amused, taking his arm.

"Following us for lack of a better lead I see."

"Of course not. I'm hopelessly infatuated with you if you must know."

"I knew it all along."

"Well, more truthfully, I was hoping to enchant you out of the nugget of information that brings you here."

"I may be persuaded to listen to your offer. What are you hungry for?"

She pursed her lips, mocking thought with a bit of mischief in her eye. "House special?"

"Hmm, I believe I see one of those across the street behind those café curtains."

"Ever the clever devil, Beau Longstreet."

"Clever? No. Enchanting?"

"We shall see."

The house special happened to be roast pork, mashed potatoes with a rich brown gravy, fresh beans, and enough wine to mellow the conversation.

"So what is it? What brings you here?" Samantha said around a forkful of chocolate cake.

"Enchanted yet?"

"That remains to be seen."

"I feel enchanted."

"Then give me what I want."

"Don't you want to finish your cake first?"

She feigned irritation. "Information, please."

"Well if you must know. Our bondswoman made an appearance at Nebraska First Bank. Sheriff Basset received a dodger from the league and tipped off both banks in town. The cashier tried to stall her long enough for an arrest but she became skittish and bolted. We've got the second bank under surveillance, but frankly my gut tells me she's gone."

She wiped a bit of chocolate frosting from her lip. "Enchanted."

He held her chair. "I much prefer this exchange to Kingsley."

CHAPTER EIGHTEEN

New York

Gould sat in his spacious darkened office shadowed in the halo of a single desk lamp. He read the Salmon Chase statement of the blind trust account. He glanced at his desk calendar and drummed the desk with his fingers. *Too slow. What's taking so long? El Anillo was expensive, but normally the Don's ring could be counted on for swift efficiency. The delays are unacceptable.*

He reached for a cut-glass decanter on his credenza and poured a stiff measure of cognac. He swirled the amber liquid in soft light refracted in the facets of the elegant tumbler. He sampled the bouquet. Excellent. A soft sip burned, mellowed, and warmed its way to satisfaction.

It is time for the Counselor to make his displeasure known. The Don must speed up the redemptions. The Missouri Pacific opportunity could not wait. The longer it took to liquidate the latter, the more likely the game would be found out. There was, of course, no way this gambit could be traced to him. He'd taken great pains in that regard. No, it was simply about the money. The money and winning at all cost.

Santa Fe

Don Victor read the telegram by firelight, warming himself at the hearth. He disliked written communication even when veiled as this one. Communications depending on third persons like telegraphers or messengers served only to complicate matters.

Client displeased at slow rate of progress.

Who the hell did this arrogant hombre think he took for his displeasure? El Anillo could snuff out the man like a candle. He clenched his jaw. He could not even answer his own question. He didn't know who the client was, arrogant or not. What's more, this client paid handsomely. He dropped the telegram into the fire. He would see what Escobar could do to speed up collections.

San Francisco

The Stanford came as a pleasant surprise. She owed the surprise, in part, to the man who chose it. One of the more elegant hotels anywhere in the west, the Stanford seemed an epicurean choice for a man who preferred a frontier brothel to conventional accommodations. She waited in the spacious marble and teak lobby seated in a Victorian wing-chair upholstered in deep forest green. A massive candlelit, crystal chandelier suspended from the two-story domed lobby sprinkled soft light across the polished black marble floor. Quiet conversational furnishings were grouped at intervals around the perimeter, leaving the central reception expanse open from the massive front entrance with its uniformed attendant; in the reception area stood a polished wood registration desk, flanked by sweeping circular staircases ascending to guest rooms on the upper floors. A single polished round table stood beneath the chandelier, its center occupied by a massive oriental vase filled with an explosion of fresh multicolored flowers that scented the air with the barest hint of tropical fragrance.

The luxury seemed in order. They'd made off with a rather substantial sum of money in a rather short period of time. It felt good to relax a little without looking over her shoulder for the handsome detective or some of his more rustic associates. The puzzling part was how quickly law enforcement caught on to their activities. Given the distances, the time that would be taken to discover the forgeries and the speed they were traveling, it should have taken longer. They should have been able to pass the whole lot, or most of it, before they were found out.

Approaching footfalls drew her attention across the lobby. Escobar's dark eyes flicked from side to side on the edge of alert. The trappings of respectability did not rule out the possibility of a trap. He nodded.

"Señorita."

"Señor."

He tilted his chin to an arch near the front entrance. "May I suggest the salon? We should find a place of private conversation there."

She nodded and followed. The salon resembled a library. Book-lined shelves muted conversational groupings of velvet-covered furnishings discreetly scattered around the room. Low lamplight turned the sitting areas into inviting islands of light. He led her to a back corner table with facing chairs. He held the first for her before taking his. A black man in a white coat appeared at his side.

"May I offer you an aperitif?"

"Agave."

His manners went only so far.

"And for the lady?"

"Sherry."

The waiter disappeared.

He drew a cheroot from his pocket and bit the tip. He scratched a match with a thumbnail, cupped the thin cigar, and drew it to light. He flicked out the match behind a mask of blue smoke. "The Don is displeased. Our client grows impatient. He wants faster results. Now."

"That's fine for the Don and his client. I'm the one taking the risk."

"You are well compensated . . ." He cut himself off for the waiter.

He set the drinks before them and departed.

"You are well compensated for the risk you take. If that bargain is no longer satisfactory, we could surely make another arrangement."

The words were casual. Tight lips and a glint in his eye gave them threat. The implication was clear; one did not simply walk away from this arrangement. She fortified herself with a sip of sherry.

"So, what do you suggest?"

He paused, his glass halfway to his lips.

"We go south." He took a swallow. "To Los Angeles and San Diego, there we catch the Texas & Pacific east. We redeem the rest of the bonds on their own line. ¿Es muy bueno, no?"

"We? You mean I bank the bonds."

"Sí. This is our arrangement, no?"

Arrangement, again. "Yes."

"Then we understand one another, *comprende*?"

"What about the detectives?"

"What about them?" He knocked back his glass. "Most likely they are scratching their asses in Nebraska, wondering what happened to us. If we move fast, we should finish in El Paso. You can catch a stage to Galveston and be long gone at sea before they could possibly catch us."

"It didn't take them that long to catch on the last time. What makes you think that won't happen again?"

"Would the señor care for another tequila?"

"Sí."

"And the lady?" His smile shone bright light in the gloom.

"Please."

He vanished into shadow, but for his white coat.

"This time we will not have the misfortune of betrayal."

"What do you mean, betrayal?"

190

"It seems the engraver who produced the plates for our bonds couldn't resist making a thirteenth for himself, very unfortunate for him. He was eliminated of course, but his son could not resist his father's temptation. He attempted to cash the bond and thus alerted the authorities before we cashed our first bond."

"So that's how they caught on so quickly."

Fresh drinks arrived.

"Most unfortunate, but at least that will not happen again."

"I wonder if they know how many bonds were printed."

"Hmm." He tipped the ash from his cigar in the tray and relit it. "I doubt they know. A forger worth his salt wouldn't keep careful records of such a transaction."

"He was clever enough to skim a hundred-thousand-dollar forgery."

"A mistake for which he paid."

She took a stiff measure of sherry. "He paid before the mistake was discovered."

He cracked a half-smile, cold light in his eye. "The terms of our arrangements are often final."

Arrangements, again. The only way out of this is to finish the job. The only way to do that is to strike fast. "There is one more thing we can do to improve our chances of success."

"What is that?"

"We stay out of sight until we are ready to strike."

"Of course we stay out of sight."

"That's not what I mean. We don't cash any bonds in California until we are ready to board an eastbound Texas & Pacific train."

"But it will take time to travel there. We have opportunities in Los Angeles and San Diego."

"San Diego, maybe. Los Angeles, no. The first bond will tell those pursuing us where we are and where we are going. Once we are on the Texas & Pacific, we can finish before the first bond is redeemed."

"The Don and our client will not be pleased by further delay."

"Do they want the job finished or not? The delay won't trouble them unless you tell them what we are planning. I take the risk. You and your Don and his client get the money. If I get caught, you're in for a bigger delay than a trip to San Diego. Now what is it going to be?"

He tossed off his drink and signaled for another. "We leave in the morning."

CHAPTER NINETEEN

Omaha

Bright light splashed the white linen tableware in the hotel dining room. The welcoming smells of fresh coffee and breakfast bacon scented the air. Kingsley spooned sugar into his tea with a dash of cream. He stirred thoughtfully.

"She's not coming back, you know."

Samantha let her coffee cool. "No, I suppose not."

"No point in cooling my heels here any longer. I sent a wire off to Chicago yesterday after tea. Unless they see some reason to keep me here, I believe I shall toddle on back to Denver for the comforts of home and hearth and all that. Will you come along?"

Her lashes lifted over the rim of her cup. *Surely not you, Reggie old boy.* "Perhaps I should stay here to keep an eye on them." She tilted her head ever so slightly across the room. Cane and Longstreet settled themselves at a table.

Kingsley took his tea with a slurp. "Eye is it? On them, or is it somewhat more on him?"

"Mr. Kingsley, whatever are you suggesting?"

"Come now, Samantha, the two of you can't think you're as subtle as all that."

"I don't know what you're talking about."

He chuckled. "Please. Well, then, keep an eye on the opposition if you must, just remember who signs your pay voucher."

"That I never forget."

"We're always a step behind." Cane drummed his fingers on the breakfast table, his ham and eggs going cold on the plate.

"It's the nature of a chase when you follow someone without knowing where they are going," Longstreet said.

"That's it! Why didn't I think of it before? You're smarter than you look, Beau."

"Of course I am. What did I say?"

"We do know where they are going."

"We do? Where?"

"Come along; we need to wire Colonel Crook before we check on the bank."

Samantha sat at a window table where the

café curtains afforded her a good view of the bank across the street. She sipped coffee, waited, and watched. Cane and Longstreet arrived promptly at one o'clock as they made their afternoon rounds. Watching them had become predictably easy with the regular routines the men followed. They spent several minutes with the banker before reappearing on the boardwalk for a brief conversation. Somewhat out of habit they parted company, with Cane appearing to cross the street into the next block, while Beau turned back toward the hotel. *Curious, might something be afoot?* She resolved to watch a bit longer. Minutes passed.

"May I join you?"

She glanced up, surprised to find Longstreet standing beside the table.

"Please." She offered the chair across the gingham-checked table.

The waitress came to the table.

"Coffee."

"I'll have a warm-up too."

She went off to fetch a cup and the pot.

"Haven't seen anything of old Reggie recently."

"He's gone back to Denver."

"And you stayed here to keep an eye on us."

"On the bank."

"And us. She's not coming back."

"So Kingsley thinks."

"We're inclined to agree. Cane went off to wire Colonel Crook."

The waitress set down a fresh cup of coffee and refilled Samantha's.

"And you found yourself in desperate need of a cup of coffee."

He smiled. "No, I came by to tell you we will most likely be heading back to Denver."

"What, you're not preparing to disappear in the middle of the night?"

"As I recall, you started that."

She suppressed a smile of her own.

"I thought I'd let you know as a courtesy. You'll have time to check in with Reggie and won't be left trying to stalk us in our absence."

"Stalk! Whatever do you mean?"

"Caught in the act, though I find the idea of a beautiful woman following my every move rather pleasant."

"Don't flatter yourself."

"Sorry, I didn't mean to misread your intentions."

"Nor I yours." She held his eyes.

She scraped back her chair.

"Where are you going?"

"I need to wire Kingsley."

"Supper?"

"I'll think about it."

"Six o'clock in the lobby?"

"How can you can be so abominably certain sure of yourself?"

"Practice."

Shady Grove

I waited down the block until the last ray of sunlight disappeared behind the mountains. This had to be as early as early evening gets. It was so early, every light in the place was lit or being lit. I slipped through the front gate and kept to the shadows as far from window light as possible. I amused myself waiting for the sun to set by conjuring up a plausible reason for skulking about the grounds in the dark on the chance I should be discovered. The colonel's stories had taught me the value of a good lie. A lost watch, dropped on my earlier visit, seemed plausible enough. I moved along the north side of the home toward the back corner window that opened to the colonel's room. I hoped. The window was indeed open as expected, though I could see little more than lamplight from the ground.

"Psssst!"

A hand appeared, reaching below the sill. The fingers wiggled expectantly. I handed up the bottle. No sooner than he had it in his grip, panic set in.

"Time for supper, Colonel."

He dropped the bottle. The telltale shatter should surely have exposed me were I not somehow miraculously able to catch it.

"Can't you give me a moment here to enjoy the night air?"

I flattened against the wall below the window.

"Now, now, Colonel, you very well know the importance of maintaining a punctual schedule."

"At my age nothing could be of less import than a punctual schedule. I have my bladder and bowels to attest to that. Now, do indulge me a few moments. It's the night air for heaven's sake."

"It will still be night when you return from supper. Now, come along."

I heard the creak of the colonel's chair propelled by purposeful footfalls. Now what? I couldn't possibly wait here until he returned from supper. Penny would be waiting. The best I could do was to return the following afternoon. He'd be salty for missing his daily ration of grog, though it seemed a small price for preserving the secrecy of our little arrangement. That settled it, at least for my part. I tucked the bottle away in my coat and started back to the front gate only to be confronted by a new unforeseen development.

A monstrous full moon appeared over the treetops flooding the yard in bright light. I had no shadow to cling to in making my way to the gate. I'd just as well cross the yard in full view of the house. I paused at the corner, staring across the manicured lawn like a no-man's-land surrounding a place of imprisonment. The moon was certain to draw attention. I was certain to be seen. Now what? Of course, a thespian to play the part.

I crouched behind the shrubbery backing the flower beds along the front of the home, taking care to stay below the windows until I reached the walkway to the front door. I studied the doors and windows. I couldn't see anyone. I fished my lost watch out of my pocket and closed it in my fist where it could easily be found at just the right moment. I stepped onto the walkway and bent low, studying the grass as I slowly followed the path to the gate.

"You there! Is something the matter?"

I bent down and recovered my watch. I turned to the challenger and recognized the gardener silhouetted in overalls and slouch hat.

"No, nothing now. It's Robert Brentwood.

I lost my watch on my earlier visit with Colonel Crook. I've just found it." I held it up to the light.

"Ah, Mr. Brentwood, glad you found it."

"Thank you. Have a pleasant evening."

I turned out the gate and started for home. I glanced at my watch. Just enough time to stash the colonel's bottle and pick up Penny without being terribly late. It might be wise to apologize for being a little late, having gone back to Shady Grove to look for my watch.

It wasn't my habit to visit Colonel Crook on Sunday. Penny had the day off and we'd taken to spending those free days together. I made allowance for needing to have him clarify a point in the story I was unable to decipher from my notes. We agreed to meet for an early supper. I arrived at Shady Grove soon after lunch much to the colonel's surprise.

"Robert," he beamed as the attendant wheeled him out to the veranda. "I hadn't expected to see you today."

I rose from my seat in greeting. "I wasn't quite finished with where we left off yesterday. I thought I might impose on you to finish our business today."

"Imposition, nothing of the sort, I'm

delighted to see you."

"I'm sure." I winked as the attendant, a dour stocky old thing, strode away.

He smiled, hand out for the bottle. "Now, where were we?"

"Cane wired you concerning the surveillance in Omaha."

"Ah, yes. Two points there. The first rather brilliant."

"You mean about knowing where the forgers were headed."

"Indeed. Cane deduced that much of their advantage had to do with the time it took for the bonds to be redeemed. He spotted a weakness in their scheme."

"What was that?"

"Continental Express cashed the bonds. All we needed to do was enlist their cooperation and the losses would cease."

"And did you?"

"After a fashion. Continental Express responded to my query. They were willing to assist us, but were somewhat limited in their ability to do so. It seems Continental Express money orders were sold by sales agents. They agreed to notify their agents by letter to be on the lookout for letters of credit in large denominations, but couldn't commit to any more than that."

"That seems as though it might have

helped."

"Too slow I'm afraid, by letter I mean."

"And the second point?"

"They'd further concluded the woman wasn't coming back. I instructed them to return to Denver. Somewhat later we learned she went straight to the depot following her encounter with the first Omaha banker and surreptitiously decamped for parts unknown."

CHAPTER TWENTY

Denver

Longstreet walked the quiet, tree-lined street to the wrought-iron gate. He'd spent so little time at Maddie O'Rourke's rooming house it didn't yet feel like home. He climbed the steps to the front porch and paused at the door. He did have a room. Then again he'd been away long enough to feel the need of an introduction. He tapped on the knocker. Moments later heels clicked toward the door. She smiled at the sight of him.

"Beau, I'd all but given up and re-rented your room."

"It's been a long and rather involved assignment."

"Come in, come in. You know you live here. You don't have to knock."

"It's been so long I didn't want to startle anyone."

"Very considerate of you, welcome back."

Her greeting and the familiar smell of freshly baked bread and wax floor polish did have the feeling of home after all.

"Were you able to bring your assignment to a successful conclusion?"

"I'm afraid not. We've more work to do, but for the moment the trail's gone cold."

"You must be exhausted from your journey. Why don't you freshen up and you can tell us all about it over supper."

"Six-thirty sharp."

"And you remember the rules. Splendid!"

Longstreet presented himself in the dining room, just as Maddie set out platters of fried chicken with biscuits, gravy, and sweet-sour stewed greens. Mrs. Fitzwalter greeted him with a nod.

"Welcome back, Mr. Longstreet."

"Thank you, Mrs. Fitzwalter. Please call me Beau. I seem to have won over Maddie here, I wouldn't want undue formality to set her back."

She laughed girlishly. "Beau it is then and Abigail for me."

With that a tall gaunt scarecrow of a man wearing a dark frock coat and gray pants came in. "Richard Brighton." He extended a bony hand.

"Beau Longstreet."

"Nice to meet you, Mr. Longstreet. I was beginning to wonder if these ladies had made you up out of whole cloth. I missed your arrival and that's been the lot of it."

"Occupational hazard, my comings and goings can be somewhat irregular."

"Well, good to have you back at last. By my count, Maddie, that puts us one room away from a full house."

"It does, Richard. Now if you'll all be seated we should eat this before it gets cold."

Conversation fell to passing, ladling, cutting, and such.

"Maddie tells us you're a detective, Beau," Brighton said. "That sounds like exciting and perhaps dangerous work."

"It can be. It can also be tediously dull, waiting for events to develop. We've had plenty of that in this last assignment."

Maddie tilted her chin, curious. "Are you at liberty to discuss the nature of the assignment?"

"I shan't go into specifics, but in general it is a rather sophisticated counterfeit scheme with substantial sums of money involved."

"Oh, my, the criminal mind astounds with its capacity for nefarious shenanigans," Abigail said.

"Are these people dangerous?" Maddie asked.

"We've had a couple of scrapes."

"Scrapes?"

"An ambush. Oh, and my partner, Briscoe Cane, woke up to a dusty gray in his hotel room."

"A snake!" Maddie gasped.

"The worst kind," Brighton said. "Was he hurt?"

"Fortunately, no."

"For a mercy, Beau, how do you manage it?" Maddie's eyes held his wide.

"Part of the job."

"Thank you no, not for me. We've peach pie for dessert." She rose and began clearing the dishes.

Longstreet stood and stacked Brighton's place setting with his.

"Beau, please sit. That's my job."

"I must have missed the rule that says I can't help."

She started for the kitchen; her eyes smiled.

Cane sat at his corner table in the Silver Slipper studying amber light filtered through a glass of whiskey. He couldn't shake the feeling they were missing something. These people didn't just disappear like so much smoke in the wind. They knew pursuit was on to them. They'd reversed their pattern the moment they felt pressured. Where did they go after Omaha? Neither north nor south seemed promising. Towns with banks followed the rails. It had to be east or west. What would he do? He tossed off his drink and poured another. The light remained amber.

Time, he'd put distance and time between passing a bond and the discovery it was a forgery. East would shorten the distance the bond had to travel and hasten discovery. West, of a surety they'd gone west. Would they resume their former pattern? Not likely, Crook had league members all along the Union Pacific line. They'd find no more success at that than they had in Omaha. They couldn't know that. Or could they? They were clever. The league had no reports of attempts to negotiate bonds responding to the dodger. They hadn't even attempted to pass one. More than likely they'd gone to ground somewhere to let things cool off. Time and distance, time and distance, that is the key, but the key to where? West he could say with some confidence. How far? Where would they next strike; or would they? They'd already made off with a handsome sum. Could it be the game was over?

Could their adversaries have made off with a small fortune never to be seen again? Possible but his gut told him no. That argument had one flaw. Small didn't satisfy fortune for this brand of criminal.

Chapter Twenty-One

The stage rocked south, the monotony of chocking dust and heat broken occasionally by majestic coastal vistas blue and golden to the very rim of the earth. Cecile steeled herself against the pockmarked ferret dozing across the coach. The run south forced them into prolonged close contact, uncomfortably close. The shadow of their *arrangement* lurked behind those black darting eyes. *Our terms are often final.* She was a convenience to be discarded the moment her usefulness ceased. She held her purse in her lap, never far from her pearl-handled .32 caliber revolver. Should the need arise, she would require a fast well-placed shot.

Fortunately, at least for the trip to Los Angeles, they traveled with a drummer of somewhat cordial demeanor. The good fellow made no secret of his interest in an attractive companion. She used that casually at rest stops and the like to maintain some distance from Escobar who seemed mildly annoyed though not overly so. She suspected the intruder irritated his expectation of control over the situation. Should he decide to terminate their association, he would have to deal with the untidy matter of a witness. Perhaps she made too much of her discomfort with her employer's intentions, but her instincts in the matter were quite keen. Better to be on edge and judge the risk in retrospect than find oneself fatally overconfident.

"Monterey station," the driver called from the box. "Thirty-minute rest stop." The coach slowed to a stop. The driver climbed down to open the coach door. He helped Cecile down to the dusty plaza fronting an adobe and tile-roofed station set against a panoramic ocean view. A fresh breeze cooled the day's heat, lightening her mood.

"The view from the back patio is breathtaking," the drummer said. "May I show you?"

"Why, that would be lovely." She accepted his arm, noticing the cool. Was it the breeze or the glare at her back? She paid it no heed allowing him to lead her through the station's tiled common room to a back patio overlooking the ocean. Thirty minutes reprieve from her constant companion was both welcome and brief.

"Oh, my yes, it's lovely. Do you pass this way often?"

"Every couple of months. My business takes me to Los Angeles several times a year."

"What sort of business are you in, if you don't mind my asking?"

"Export import. Primarily goods from the Orient."

"That sounds exciting."

"It can be. And you? What brings you here?"

"Family business. I'm settling my father's estate."

"I see. And your traveling companion?"

"The family attorney." She glanced over her shoulder to make sure he hadn't followed them. "Wretched little man, but quite good at what he does."

"I see. Will you be staying in Los Angeles?"

"No. I'm afraid we are traveling on to San Diego."

"Pity. I should have enjoyed the opportunity to have a more fulsome acquaintance."

"Yes, that might have been nice. Perhaps on our return."

"Perhaps."

The gold-lettered sign in the window read California Harbor Bank. The spacious lobby smelled new with that subtle hint of currency that said bank. A few early customers stood at teller windows conducting the routine business of banking. Her purpose would require somewhat more than routine. He was easy to find. There must be some unwritten rule about the organization of bank lobbies. The cashier's desk invariably flanked the vault, which stood open when the bank opened for business. The cashiers always wore some dark suit with a bearing that bespoke reserved confidence and security. Mostly they were old, cashier being a position of responsibility and authority. It took a banker years to rise to such a position of trust. This one was not, old that is. *Interesting.*

She approached the railing separating the vault from the lobby. The railing must be another part of the code. As a barrier, it was useless. It did suffice to demark the inner sanctum of authority from simple depository transactions. He looked up. Clear gray eyes smiled. He rose, tall and handsome too.

"May I help you?"

"I'd like to speak with the cashier."

He rounded the desk and swept the gate open with a slight bow of his head. "Myles Lamont, at your service, Miss."

"St. James, Cecile St. James." The head bow took her in head to toe.

"Please come in, Miss St. James. Have a seat."

He showed her to a side chair and held it for her. The exaggerated courtesy saw her comfortably seated. He returned to his chair.

"Now, Miss St. James, it is miss, isn't it?"

She nodded, suppressing a smile. *Well this is a first.*

"How may I be of service?"

She drew the folded bond from her purse and slid it across the desk. "I should like to pledge this as collateral against a letter of credit."

He glanced at the bond, a brow lifted in surprise. "That's a rather substantial sum. May I ask the purpose?"

"I intend to purchase some land."

"Rather a lot of land I should think, unless you've discovered gold or something."

She returned his gaze. "Let's just say a large parcel for now."

"In the area?"

"Nearby."

"You're new to San Diego."

"I am."

"Then on behalf of the bank let me welcome you to San Diego."

"Thank you. Now, about the letter, a Texas & Pacific bond is as good as gold. How long will it take to secure it?"

"No more than a couple of days. I shall need to consult one or two of the directors before negotiating a sum this large. It's Monday, shall we say Wednesday afternoon?"

"If you say so."

"Should any questions arise, where may I contact you?"

"I'm staying at the Paradise Hotel."

"Ah, of course, the very best. Their dining room is one of the finest restaurants in San Diego. Have you tried it?"

"Not yet." She made it less a statement than an invitation.

"Would you care to join me this evening?"

"Why, Mr. Lamont, are you sure? We've only just met."

"Of course I'm sure, that is, if you'd do me the honor."

She colored a trifle. A useful skill she'd acquired for such situations. "This evening then."

"Splendid. I shall call for you at seven."

"Seven it is."

■ ■ ■ ■

Candlelit tables created islands glittering in cut crystal, fine china, and silver set against a subdued background of dark wood and green velvet. Here and there pastoral scenes painted in oil graced the walls flanked by trimmed sconces. The wait staff in starched white jackets floated among the tables serving the diners over the quiet hum of muted conversation. The chief steward, who greeted Lamont by name, showed them to a corner table. He seated Cecile, distributed menus, and summoned a waiter. She opened the menu. Hers had no prices.

"May I serve you an aperitif, Mr. Lamont?"

"Yes, Justin. Miss St. James?"

"Please call me Cecile. Dry sherry please."

"I'll have the same, Justin."

"Very good, sir."

He smiled. "Then you must call me Myles."

"What do you recommend?"

"The fish is fresh and the steaks are also very good."

"Fresh fish, one should take advantage of that."

"It is one of the benefits of living by the

sea. Hopefully you will have time to enjoy that while you attend to your land investments. I must say, such a large commitment is remarkable."

"Remarkable for a woman you mean."

Caught, he hesitated as the waiter arrived with their drinks.

"I didn't say that."

"You thought it."

"How do you know?"

"It was written all over your face. Now, my turn, how does someone as young as you rise to the position of cashier in a bank?"

"It's simple really. All you need is a father who owns the bank."

She laughed. "You're honest. I like that."

"Good, I'm glad." He lifted his glass. "Then let's drink to your success as a land baroness."

"A prosperous banker's son who bestows royal titles, I should never have believed it. Don't you think that toast a bit premature?"

"Not after I talk to Father."

"Ah, now that we must drink to."

"Do you think that is wise? Do you plan to defraud this banker or bed him?" Escobar's question hung icy over the sun-warmed breakfast table.

"We had dinner. Not that it is any business of yours. What's more, I shall see him again this evening."

"It is my business, until our arrangement is finished."

Arrangement, again. The implied threat grew tiresome. She felt the weight of the pistol in the bag on her lap. He saw their arrangement on his terms. She understood a second set of terms. Should she choose to terminate the arrangement, she could cash one last bond for her trouble. She smiled. The strength of her position depended on the weasel's unchallenged machismo.

"The banker is part of our arrangement. You may not like it, but his father owns the bank. If he finds me attractive, it serves only to assure us that we shall have our letter of credit. Would you have me brush off his attentions and risk insulting him?"

No answer.

"I thought not." Insulting the male pride he understood. *Men.* So simple really.

Myles Lamont was a man accustomed to getting what he wanted. By the time port was served his appetite had sharpened. She could read him like an open book. Under other circumstances she might have easily captivated him. She had a good start and it was only the end to a second casual dinner. What might life be? Wife to a prosperous banker. He'd not remain dashing and handsome. Charming perhaps, though familiarity had a way of exacting its wage. He'd grow paunchy, hair thinning in time. She'd become a comfortable matron of San Diego society, pampered, enjoying her husband's wealth. So long as nothing of her past came out. And that of course is the nasty little secret, her past. Choices. Life is full of them.

"We should have everything wrapped up by lunchtime tomorrow."

She blinked.

"I say, have you heard a word I've said?"

"Yes, of course. I'm sorry. Just a little preoccupied."

"So am I. Let's hope for the same reason."

She favored him with a smoky smile. "And what might that be?"

"I think you know very well what that might be."

"I do." She let her eyes drift half-closed and held out her glass. "Another port and you may escort me to my room."

He poured.

Choices. Pity crime pays so well.

She waved goodbye. He smiled *until then* across the lobby. She left the bank, the letter of credit safely tucked away in her purse. Myles expected he'd see her for supper and somewhat more for a third consecutive evening. She wouldn't make it. She'd be on the morning stage eastbound to Yuma. He'd been charming company and great fun, soft clay in her hands. He was well on the way to falling in love with her. A wealthy banker's wife, the idea had never crossed her mind before Myles. She might have considered it, if it hadn't been for her current arrangement. She had no choice but to finish this business. With luck she'd escape her employer and the authorities.

The brothel Escobar selected for his accommodation was located in a seedy part of town near the harbor. The saloons and whorehouses there catered to travelers and seamen alike. Prim and properly dressed as she was she made stark contrast to the painted ladies lounging about the parlor. The madam who greeted her summoned a dark-eyed waif to show her to Escobar's room.

The girl regarded her with suspicion, puzzling over why the ferret-like Mexican would take a crib in the house and send for a girl like this. She'd seen some unusual appetites in her time, been party to a few, but she couldn't recall anything like this.

She led the way up a creaky stairway to a dingy second-floor corridor, dimly lit by a single window at the far end. The girl stopped at a room midway down the threadbare carpet and inclined her head to the door. Without further word she made her way back down the hall toward the parlor

Cecile knocked. A muffled ruffle sounded within.

"Come in."

A frowzy redhead sat on the bed wrapped in the flimsy suggestion of a robe. Escobar lay on the bed covered in a sheet.

"Be a good girl and give us a minute." He patted her bottom.

The springs squeaked. Cecile stepped aside. The girl let herself out.

"Did you get it?"

She opened her purse and tossed the letter on the bed. She had no intention of getting close enough to hand it to him.

He snatched it up for a cursory glance. "Took you long enough."

"I'm on my way to Yuma."

"I'll find you there in a few days."

CHAPTER TWENTY-TWO

Denver

They finished the breakfast dishes on a bright Saturday morning. Lately he'd taken to wiping in spite of her protests. She'd be loathe to admit it, but she did enjoy his company and didn't mind the help, either. Saturdays were a bit more leisurely with no need of Beau running off to work. This day, Mr. Brighton was away on a business trip, leaving the house to the three of them. Beau folded the towel.

"Now about supper this evening," he said. "Is there something special you would like?"

"As a matter of fact there is. I'd like to take you out to supper."

"What, you don't care for my cooking?"

He raised his hands in mock surrender. "Heavens no, I merely thought to treat you to an evening away from the kitchen."

"Perhaps you've forgotten my house rule,

no fraternization."

"I wasn't suggesting anything so bold. I was merely suggesting supper."

She blushed. He had a maddening way of twisting her meaning in ways she didn't intend. She had her standards. She was entitled to them. Why was it he felt compelled to ignore them when it came to things like clearing the table? Why did she let him? Because he was such a damnably charming and handsome brute.

"What is to become of Mrs. Fitzwalter?"

"You've food in the house. She's an able-bodied adult. I should think if properly forewarned, she shouldn't starve."

Her nose wrinkled with a throaty laugh. "You are incorrigible."

"Is that good?"

"It might be."

He considered the dining room at the Palace Hotel and decided against it. He thought it too ostentatious not to mention the association with a hotel. He had no intention of crowding her good humor on either account. Delmonico's made a quiet comfortable alternative. She looked lovely as she swept into the parlor from her quarters somewhere at the back of the house. Her hair swept up in auburn curls fired in lamplight and tied with a ribbon to match her emerald green gown. She'd taken his arm on the short walk to the restaurant as naturally as drawing a breath. The waiter showed them to a candlelit corner table and seated Maddie. He handed them each a menu.

"May I offer you something to drink?"

"I'm not sure. As I recall the rules, the lady there is the judge of moderation."

She pulled an exaggerated scowl. "Oh, please. Have you an Irish whiskey?"

"Indeed we do."

"Neat if you please."

"Very good, madam. And you, sir?"

"Make it two."

The waiter turned to the bar.

"Whiskey, I'm impressed."

"I am an Irish lass."

"Indeed you are."

The waiter returned with their glasses. "I'll give you a few moments to look over the menu."

Longstreet lifted his glass. "To a lovely Irish lass."

She colored. "Spare us the silver-tongued blarney." She toasted the rim of his glass and took a swallow.

They passed a pleasant supper with wine and cherry pie for dessert. The walk home was pleasant too, aglow with moderation. Maddie let them in the front door.

"Would you care for a cup of coffee?"

"I would."

She lit a lamp in the parlor and took herself off to the kitchen, leaving Beau to his thoughts. He took a seat on the settee.

There was something about Maddie O'Rourke. Something he couldn't quite put his finger on. He felt comfortable with her. He'd never thought of an attractive woman as comfortable before. What did that mean? Why would he think such a thing? She was comfortable with herself, that's why. He enjoyed crowding the observance of all her strict rules on decorum. He'd already ruffled a few of those rules so far with this evening. Yet she seemed not to mind. He poked fun at her and she found humor in it. *Comfortable,* that must be it.

She carried two steaming cups of coffee into the parlor and set them on the table before the settee and took a seat. She picked up a cup and blew gently over the steaming surface and took a small sip.

"Pleasant end to a lovely evening. I must say I haven't enjoyed myself that much in a long time."

"Now there's a pity. Life has so much to offer if you only give it the chance."

"Yes, I suppose that's true. It's only that after Matthew passed away I haven't had much reason to give it the chance."

"Perhaps you should think about giving it a try."

She arched a brow. "Waxing philosophical or volunteering are we?"

"Sorry, none of my business really." He retreated to his coffee cup.

"Don't be sorry, Beau. I didn't mean that the way it sounded. You pushed me out of my nest. I had a wonderful time. It just made me a little uncomfortable."

"Good."

"Why is that good?"

"Because you had a wonderful time. Interesting, really."

"How so?"

"While you were making the coffee, I was thinking that I had a wonderful time because you made me feel comfortable. Now you say you had a wonderful time and it made you uncomfortable."

"There you go with that silver-tongued blarney again. You can't fool me, Beau Longstreet. I know your kind."

"You doubt my sincerity? I am cut to the quick."

"Don't be silly." She gathered up the cups and took them to the kitchen.

He stood waiting at the foot of the stairs to his room. She paused as she passed on the way to the back of the house.

"I did have a wonderful time."

He lifted her chin, her eyes green liquid in the dim light of the parlor lamp. He kissed her ever so softly.

"I too had a wonderful time, no blarney about it."

She returned his kiss.

"Now you've made me uncomfortable. I'll turn out the lamp. You run along before I'm accused of undue fraternization." He watched her go, then huffed out the lamp.

She blew out the bedside lamp and slipped between the sheets. *Beau Longstreet. Don't be a fool, girl. You know the type. He says I make him feel comfortable. That makes me uncomfortable. He kissed me and that made me less uncomfortable. I kissed him and that makes him uncomfortable. I haven't felt that kind of comfort in . . . a long, long time. I have my standards. I do. Don't I?*

Shady Grove

The following Saturday found the colonel waiting for me as he warmed himself in the still morning air on the veranda. He glanced up at the sound of my approach and furrowed his brow. I sensed he read my mood as I drew up a chair.

"Robert."

I nodded.

"You seem a bit dour for such a splendid morning."

"I suppose I am the least bit dour."

"No trouble in paradise I trust?"

"No. It's the book."

"Ah ha, I sense a rejection."

"Indeed. Polite, but rejected nonetheless."

"I'm sorry. I don't know much about these things, but isn't rejection a rather common matter of form?"

"They say. I suppose it is, until it happens to you."

"Is it well written?"

"They say I show some aptitude."

"The story then?"

"It's a damn fine story. You know that."

"Then you still believe in your endeavor."

"I do."

"Good. Then show a bit of that fiery determination of yours. I'll wager this one isn't the only publishing house in New York."

"It isn't."

"Then buck up, lad. You've only to try another."

"I shall. It's only the matter of what I

should tell Penny."

"Why, tell her the truth of course."

"But I feel as though I failed her."

"How could such a modest setback possibly have failed her?"

"We were hoping . . ."

"I see. This romance of yours is progressing toward some more permanent arrangement then."

"How could you know?"

"It's written all over your hangdog face, boy. Does she share your feelings for her?"

I nodded.

"Then I doubt she will feel failed. Pick yourself up. Square those shoulders and set about the business of soliciting another publishing house. You're pursuing a dream. It's a quest. Only fairy tales are free of disappointment. Now pick up your pencil and let us continue while I still have wit enough to remember this story. Where were we?"

"Longstreet and Cane had returned to Denver to await developments."

"Ah yes, I remember the morning, much as glorious as this one. Cane came into the office deep in concentration. I watched him pace. He'd stare out the window, fingering the whisker stubble on his chin. The man possessed extraordinary deductive powers.

I've mentioned my belief he could follow a fart in a snowstorm. You could almost hear his brain thrashing at the problem . . ."

Chapter Twenty-Three

"Texas & Pacific, it has to be." Cane said it to no one in particular.

"What has to be?"

"Texas & Pacific, the next run of bonds." He crossed the office on long strides like a predator preparing to pounce.

"What makes you think so?"

"They've gone to ground because we were getting too close. They're not done. I'll wager odds on that. They'll want to move fast once they start passing their paper again as they know we'll pick up their trail once the bonds begin being presented for redemption. They need a string of banks much like those along the Union Pacific. What's the next most likely?"

"The answer is printed on the bonds, Texas & Pacific."

"Notify the league members from El Paso to Yuma, no make that San Diego. Have them alert their banks. I can't say when or where, but I've a strong hunch they'll show up somewhere out there next."

"I shall alert the members today. Now here's the next problem for you to deduce. We know the woman. She does the leg work. We know she is working with someone. That person may or may not be the brains behind this operation. We can't rule out whoever that is, but given the sophistication of these criminals I would expect her contact is another low-level operative. The question is, when we do come onto them again, how do we get them to lead us to the big fish?"

"It is a good question. Let me enjoy the last deduction before you spoil my lunch with this new one."

"Right. After lunch then, don't let any grass grow underfoot."

Yuma, Arizona Territory

Dusty desert patched in dull green rolled by the eastbound stage. Escobar watched, unable to sleep. Giant saguaro cactus stood by, arms raised in surrender to the ravages of waterless heat. They surrendered and survived. Out here a man who surrendered died. He carried the California Harbor Bank letter of credit folded in his case. He would cash it at the Yuma Continental Express office, pick up another letter from the woman, and move on to Tucson. He wired Don Victor from San Diego; the cryptic message simply read *Eastbound.* He signed it *E.* The Don would not be pleased at the delay, but at least the news showed progress. The proceeds would soon flow again.

Squat adobe huts dotted the desert, signaling their approach into Yuma, which served as a gateway to California, crossing the Colorado River. The rail bridge now under construction would make Yuma an important hub, crossing Arizona on the westbound leg to the sea. Yuma also played host to an army post and the infamous territorial prison. Escobar had no wish to encounter any of that. He would conduct his business, enjoy a good Mexican meal and the higher quality tequila served here near the border. A good night's sleep or perhaps an energetic señorita and he'd be gone again by morning.

The stage crossed the Colorado, quiet and muddy at this season of the year, passable by ferry. The outskirts of town scrolled past the windows. Quiet, baked-block adobe structures reflected the afternoon heat in shimmering waves.

The driver hauled lines. The team slowed. The coach bounced and lurched to a stop.

Escobar stepped down at the station to a hot dry gust of wind. Heat reflected from the dusty street as he waited for his bag to come off the boot, brushing away a fly. He collected his small bag and crossed the street to the depot. She stepped out of the shaded porch, sheltering waiting passengers. She acknowledged him with a slight nod, indicating things had gone smoothly.

He entered the depot through the muted passenger lounge and out to the bright sunlit street beyond. He turned east on Gila Avenue to the Yuma Hotel. Thick adobe walls cooled the lobby to a tolerable warmth. He would have preferred staying at a favored brothel. The message that awaited him at registration could not be entrusted to the integrity of such an establishment even if he could have convinced the woman to leave it there. Honor among thieves went only so far. He could visit the brothel when smaller sums were involved.

He signed the register and folded the Yuma letter of credit into his case along with the Harbor Bank letter. He'd cash this one in Tucson in two days' time.

Denver
Samantha arrived in Denver bone weary from the stage ride down from Cheyenne.

233

She indulged herself with a room at the Palace, a bath, and some supper. She woke with the sun full up, dressed, and set off for the Pinkerton office. She found Kingsley ensconced at a back corner desk bathed in bright sunlight, streaming through a large window at his back. He greeted her with a nod.

"Miss Maples, welcome to Denver. Ran out of Longstreet observations I presume. When did you get in?"

"Last night."

"You don't seem much the worse for wear, considering that bloody awful stage ride in from Cheyenne."

"Trains aren't all that pleasant, but a few hours on a stagecoach is certain to improve one's appreciation for rail service. What is going on with our counterfeiters?"

"Nothing I'm afraid. Have a seat."

He indicated a hard-backed chair reminiscent of a horsehair padded stage seat absent the horsehair pad. The bath helped. It hadn't soothed two days' bone rocking on the dust-choked stage road to Denver.

"We've had no reports from the client or Chicago," Kingsley said.

"You don't suppose they've taken their haul and made off with it?"

"Hmm, that's possible of course, though I

tend to doubt it. Someone's gone to a great deal of trouble to put this caper together. The plates alone for the quality of forgery we've observed require a work of art by a gifted craftsman and a corrupt one at that. Artisans like that don't grow on trees. When you pay them off the way this lot did, I should think they would want a greater return on the gambit. No, more likely they felt the heat and have gone to ground to let their trail cool off."

"So then what are we to do?"

"We do what all good investigators do. We wait."

"Well I can't wait indefinitely at the Palace room rates, unless of course you'd be persuaded to offer me a substantial increase in compensation."

He chuckled. "By Jove, there's a good one."

"I'll take that for a no. Do you have any suggestions as to where I might find more reasonable accommodations?"

"I'm told the Widow O'Rourke runs a respectable rooming house. It's only a few blocks from here."

"I'm sure I can find it."

"Do that, and I shall keep my eye out for an assignment that gives you something to do while we wait."

"That would be the eye that never sleeps."

"I say, I see your wit has survived your travels in good order."

She found O'Rourke House on a quiet, tree-lined street. A stately three-story white-washed Victorian with neatly trimmed gardens beckoned behind a wrought-iron fence. The gate welcomed her with a groan. She marched briskly up the front walk to the porch and rapped on the door. Moments later a shadow moved beyond the lace curtains, tapping its way to the door. The shadow emerged from behind the open door, an attractive woman with auburn hair, green eyes, and a splash of freckles across an upturned nose.

"May I help you?"

"Mrs. O'Rourke?"

"Yes."

"Samantha Maples." She extended her hand. "I'm told you may have a room for rent."

"I may."

"I've only just moved to Denver and was hoping to find respectable housing. Your home came highly recommended."

"May I ask by whom?"

"Reginald Kingsley."

"Well I'm indebted to Mr. Kingsley,

though I can't say I know the name. Please come in. I've one room left. It's a little on the small side, but comfortable. If you'd like to see it, I'd be happy to show you."

"Oh, yes, please."

"Right this way then."

Samantha took in the parlor and dining room, following the widow up the center stairs to the second floor. Widow hadn't conjured up the thought of a woman near her own age. Then again in the west, tragedy could find one at any age. She turned back toward the front of the house at the landing. A window at the end of a short hallway overlooked the front walk. A door on the left led to a sunny room furnished with a bed, wardrobe, feinting couch, and a small writing table and chair.

"As I said, a little on the small side, but comfortable. Mrs. Fitzwalter has the room across the hall. My two gentlemen in residence are on the third floor. Both of them travel on business so we don't have an abundance of comings and goings. Everyone is expected to observe the house rules."

"House rules?"

"Yes. Breakfast is served at seven, dinner at six thirty. No guests of the opposite sex beyond the parlor. No gambling or late night carousing on the premises. Strong drink is permitted only in moderation and I am the judge of moderate. I shouldn't think those last two would trouble you over much. They're more for the gentlemen. The fraternization rules serve to benefit all of us in keeping the house respectable."

"I see that." *Kingsley didn't tell me the woman runs a convent. Oh well, at least it will be quiet.* "How much is the room?"

"Twenty dollars a month with a one-month deposit due in advance."

"I'll take it."

Maddie watched Samantha Maples rummage in her purse. *Handsome woman, proper and respectable I should hope.* Beau Longstreet entered her mind's eye unbidden, trailing discomfort in his wake.

O'Rourke House Dining Room
Remarkable, the effect the woman had on him. Beau presented himself in the dining room promptly at six-thirty. *She runs the house like a trim ship and here I am eager to comply.* He nodded to Mrs. Fitzwalter.

"Have you met the new boarder, Mr. Longstreet?"

"We have a new boarder?"

"We do." Maddie came out of the kitchen carrying a platter of roast beef and vegetables. "And here she is now."

238

He turned. "Sam?"

"Beau?"

"What are you doing here?" they said.

"You know each other?" Maddie said, wide-eyed.

Beau found his balance. "Colleagues, we worked on a case together."

"More like competitors, I work for Pinkerton."

"You're a detective?" Maddie shook her head, attempting to clear it from the realm of surreal.

"I am."

"Isn't that somewhat, unusual?" Mrs. Fitzwalter said.

"For a woman you mean? I suppose, though Mr. Pinkerton finds a woman operative can be quite disarming."

"I'm sure you can be," Maddie said, a wry eye toward Beau.

Beau felt oddly pinched about the collar. "I didn't know you were based in Denver."

"I wasn't. I've only just arrived. Reggie suggested I find a room here. Fortunately Maddie had one to spare."

"Good old Reggie, fortunate indeed."

"Well, shall we sit down before supper gets cold?" Maddie said.

Samantha smiled. You could cut the tension with a knife. Knowing Longstreet she sensed she'd stumbled into something more here than meets the eye. This could be deliciously entertaining. *Imagine Beau Longstreet twisting like a trout on a lure.*

Maddie passed the platter to Beau. *"Colleague competitors" indeed. And to think she'd almost suspended her . . . comfort for the rogue.*

Longstreet cut a bit of roast beef. *How in hell was he supposed to get a bite of food past the knot in his collar?*

CHAPTER TWENTY-FOUR

Chicago
The Counselor inserted the small key in the lock and opened the box. The operation had seemingly ground to a halt in recent weeks. He couldn't explain it. He could only speculate they'd encountered some law enforcement complication. He'd communicated his client's displeasure to Don Victor to no visible effect. Today the box yielded an appropriately addressed brown envelope. He tore it open and examined the contents. Another money order, it seems they were back in business. He examined the envelope; the postmark read Yuma, Arizona Territory. That partially explained the delay. They'd moved off the Union Pacific line to resume operations on the Texas & Pacific itself. He smiled at the irony. *Imagine that. How convenient. The railroad hastening its own fleecing.*

He closed the box and crossed the sunlit

marble floor to a courtesy counter. He posted the money order to his client's trust account. With luck, the operation should now complete in a few weeks. Finished, he left the post office. A pleasant day awaited, a leisurely stroll along the shore of Lake Michigan.

Denver

"Telegram for Colonel Crook."

The sober young lad presented himself at the office all businesslike in spite of bare feet and bib overalls. A shock of red hair spilled out from the brim of a comically battered straw hat. Sunburned freckled cheeks completed the effect. Were it not for the proffered yellow envelope, I should have made him in need of a fishing pole. I took the envelope and tossed him a quarter. He stuffed it in his pocket and beat a hasty retreat back to the street and one of those ungainly velocipedes he'd left parked at the boardwalk. He placed a foot on the rear peg and pushed off, vaulting onto the seat. He wheeled into traffic, made a sweeping turnabout, and set off up the street the way he'd come. I smiled at the exuberance of youth in search of his next errand. I tore open the wire.

San Diego

Alert arrived too late. California Harbor Bank accepted T&P bond.
Amount one hundred thousand. Woman decamped for parts unknown.

J. P. Cross
Sheriff
San Diego

Cane had the right of it. I turned to the map on the office wall. It dictated Yuma would be next. They'd never make it in time. It might even be too late already.

"Beau!"

Longstreet recognized a summons. He left his desk and joined Crook at the map. The colonel handed him a telegram. He read with a nod.

"Briscoe was right."

"He was."

"Now what?"

"Given what we know of these people, I expect they are eastbound on the Texas & Pacific."

"That would make Yuma next."

"My thought exactly, but you'll never get there in time. You need to round up Cane and get to El Paso as fast as you can. Hopefully the league will turn up their whereabouts by the time you arrive."

"El Paso!" Cane rubbed sleep from his eyes.

"That's what the colonel said. How do we get there?"

"Denver & Santa Fe Stage for the first leg, Butterfield has a run from Santa Fe to El Paso. Pack light and hurry. We can still make the afternoon run."

Longstreet packed in his mind as he hurried up the front walk to O'Rourke House. He mounted the porch, let himself in, and bounded up the stairs two at a time. He passed a startled Maddie cleaning on the second floor. She followed him to his room.

"What brings you home this time of day?"

He bustled about the room stuffing a bag with spare clothing. "Something's come up. Briscoe and I are leaving for El Paso this afternoon."

"El Paso? Will you be gone long?"

"Hard to say. I hope not, but one never knows in these matters." He paused to smile. "Why? Do you expect to miss me?"

"Don't flatter yourself. I simply want to know what to tell Samantha when she asks."

"And why would she do that?"

She blocked the doorway.

"Oh, come now, Beau, you don't really

expect me to settle for that 'colleagues' explanation, do you? Frankly I don't know that I'm comfortable with the situation now that she's here."

"Comfort again, we keep coming back to that, don't we?"

"Don't change the subject."

"Who's changing the subject? You brought it up. I seem to recall that my feeling comfortable with you made you uncomfortable. Samantha had nothing to do with it. Remember?"

She flushed. "Well all that's changed now, hasn't it?"

"Has it?" He dropped his bag, swept her up in his arms, and kissed her.

She fought free and slapped his face with a sharp crack.

He laughed. "You don't mean that."

"Yes, I do! I mean, I'm sorry. It's the house rules."

"Rules, rubbish." He kissed her again. She forgot to fight.

"Uncomfortable?"

She nodded.

"Me too. Now miss me until this Johnny comes marching home."

He picked up his bag and took the stairs two at a time.

She watched him go. *Miss him? Damn it!*

Samantha stormed into the Pinkerton office the following morning. Kingsley sat stirring his tea, his tweed jacket golden in bright sunlight.

"Top of the morning. You're in a bit earlier than usual."

"Longstreet's gone."

"I'm terribly sorry for your loss."

"Not that. He and Cane left for El Paso rather unexpectedly yesterday."

"Did he say why?"

"I found out at supper last night. If he told Maddie, she didn't say."

"You think it might be a development in the bogus bond case."

"It's certainly a possibility, considering they're off to El Paso."

"Why's that?"

"The Texas & Pacific Railroad."

"Yes, I suppose it could be. I'll wire Chicago to see if the client has reported anything."

Santa Fe Trail

The stage bounced and rolled, lurched and pitched, gaiting worse than a horse with one leg shorter than the rest. Cane stared out the window at choking dust clouds. Longstreet dozed in the opposite corner of the rear seat along with the snoring drummer next to him. Longstreet could sleep anywhere, probably because even when given the chance, he did precious little of that in bed.

Cane hated stage travel. They made better time than a man on horseback owing to changing teams every ten miles or so. For a man in a hurry, a stage made the fastest option when a train couldn't be had. In this job it seemed they were always in a hurry. It would help if he could sleep. He couldn't. Not for the heat, the dust, and the infernal jostling. He'd tried to read his Bible. The words bounced around his eyes like to make a man dizzy. He could recall familiar passages from memory; but actual reading came with great difficulty.

Then there was the uneasy feeling in his gut, helping keep him awake. He got them from time to time. This one might have something to do with the Wells Fargo strongbox they'd loaded in the boot before leaving Denver. The well-being of that box wasn't rightly his concern. That responsibility rested with the shotgun messenger riding up top with the driver. Cane's only connection to the box was the risk of having his travels delayed by trouble drawn to a box needing shotgun protection.

They'd made good time crossing Raton Pass on Wootton's toll road before slicing southwest on the Santa Fe Trail. With any luck they'd make Santa Fe by late afternoon tomorrow. They wouldn't get more than a few hours' break before catching the Butterfield line to El Paso. The reward for that leg would be a seat on a train somewhere west, but where? That would be up to Colonel Crook and his Great Western Detective League. They'd hit San Diego. Likely Yuma too before the league alert could put a stop to it. Tucson he'd wager if he were a wagering man. Nothing to do until then but ride it out.

The stage lurched, slamming Cane's head into the back of his seat and summarily jolting Longstreet awake.

"Whoa!" the driver called from the box. The brake engaged with a squeal.

"What the hell's goin' on?" Longstreet squinted into the dust cloud billowing past his window.

"Too early for the next rest stop," Cane said.

The coach bounced to a halt.

"Hold-up," Longstreet breathed, reaching for the pistol in his shoulder rig. "I got two over here."

The drummer slid to the floor of the coach wide-eyed.

"I got one over here," Cane said.

Longstreet cut his eyes to Cane. "They've got the drop on the driver and the shotgun messenger."

"Passengers, throw out your guns and get out of the coach now or these boys out here are dead."

"That sounds like a woman," Longstreet said.

"Don't matter. She's givin' the orders." Cane drew his Colt. He glanced at the drummer. "You heeled?" The man shook his head. "Throw your gun out, Beau. I go out this side. Make sure you can get your gun and get under the coach when I make my play. Now both of you get on out." Cane tossed his Colt out his window, opened the door, and stepped out on the driver's side, giving the bandits passengers to deal with on both sides of the coach.

"Well what have we here? Hello, handsome."

Longstreet met her smoky dark gaze over the bandana covering the rest of her face and smiled.

It is a woman. Cane held his hands in the air.

"Keep your pants on, Belle," the masked man bracing the Wells Fargo messenger and driver said. "Drop the shotgun and throw down the box."

The bandit facing down Cane leveled his gun. "You, come around the front of the coach and get on over there with them others."

Cane did as he was told, walking slowly behind the bandit's horse, forcing his minder to turn side to side in the saddle in order to keep him covered. In the instant the man turned his gaze, Cane jerked the Forehand & Wadsworth from behind his back and fired. At close range the .41 Bull Dog knocked the man from his horse. The horse bolted. Cane turned his gun to the bandit bracing the driver and shotgun messenger.

Longstreet dove to the ground, grabbed his gun, and rolled under the coach.

The drummer dove back inside the coach.

Miss dark eyes fired and fired again. Her bullets kicked up dust plumes in the road where Longstreet had been standing.

Cane ducked under the stage team. The bandit covering the box fired wildly and missed.

The masked woman wheeled her horse and raced away, followed by her partner.

Longstreet crawled out from under the stage and watched her go. *Interesting.* He holstered his gun.

The Wells Fargo man recovered his shotgun as Cane came around the front of the coach. "Much obliged to you two. You saved the company bacon this trip."

"The company can send its appreciation in care of the Great Western Detective League, Denver office."

"Detectives, I had no idea you boys was aboard. Good thing you were."

Cane retrieved his Colt and shoved the Bull Dog in the backup holster at his back. "It ain't that we don't appreciate the gratitude, but we're in kind of a hurry and this stage is late."

"Hop in," the driver said. "We're on our way."

Chapter Twenty-Five

Santa Fe

The Denver and Santa Fe stage wheeled into Santa Fe five hours late, too late to make a Butterfield connection to El Paso. That would have to wait until morning. They took rooms at the Palace Hotel over Cane's "high falutin" objection. Longstreet insisted that after three days of stage fare and two more to come they were due a real bed and a decent meal. The next morning dawned bright, hot, and dry. They made the four-block walk to the Butterfield Stage office. Cane purchased two tickets to El Paso from a clerk wearing garters to hold up his sleeves.

"We're holding a telegram for you, Mr. Cane." He handed the envelope across the counter.

Cane tore it open.

Denver

Second passed in Yuma. Proceed to Tuc-
son.

— *Crook*

He handed it to Longstreet. "Three days,
think we can get there in time?"

"Depends on how fast they're movin'. It'll
be close, I reckon."

They rolled out of Santa Fe an hour later.

Denver

The freckle-faced lad on the velocipede
rolled up to the Pinkerton office and parked
the cycle against a hitch rack. Regular rid-
ers wouldn't appreciate misappropriation of
the rack, but the lad reckoned a short stop
could do no harm. He wiped sweat from his
forehead on a tattered sleeve and bounded
up the boardwalk past the window sign
proclaiming "The Eye That Never Sleeps."

"Telegram for Mr. Kingsley."

Kingsley glanced up. "Over here, boy."

The lad crossed the office to his desk,
squinting into the bright sun streaming
through the window behind the big desk.

Kingsley took the envelope, tossed the lad
a quarter, and tore it open without noticing
the messenger or his cycle disappear the way

they'd come.

Chicago

California Harbor Bank of San Diego presented bond for collection.
                                    — *McPharlan*

"Samantha."

She left her desk at the summons. Reggie handed her the telegram. She read. "That explains El Paso. They're going to run the Texas & Pacific."

"Rather like double jeopardy, don't you think?"

"Double jeopardy?"

"Yes, using the railroad's assets to defraud itself. Not terribly sporting I should say."

Sporting. Leave it to the English.

"San Diego is old news, likely Yuma as well. Your next best chance might be Tucson."

"I'm on my way."

Samantha hurried through the front door at midmorning. Maddie set aside the bread dough, wiped her hands on her apron, and stepped into the dining room.

"What brings you home so early?"

"I need to pack," she said over her shoulder as she started up the stairs.

El Paso. Maddie followed her up the stairs to her room.

"Will you be gone long?"

"That's hard to say. Three weeks, a month, perhaps longer." She folded a fresh change of undergarments and stuffed them in a worn valise.

"Where are you going?"

"El Paso, then on to Tucson." She added another simple traveling dress and a small matching hat with a veil.

El Paso, I knew it. "My, my but you people do get around in this business."

"Can't be helped, bad people do bad things wherever they can." She closed the case, laid a finger aside her chin, and twirled around the room in thought. "Can't think of anything else at the moment. This will have to do." She picked up the case and started for the door.

"Would you like me to pack you a lunch?"

"That's very kind of you, Maddie, but I can't spare the time."

She followed her down the stairs to the door.

"Have a safe journey then and say hello to Beau if you see him."

Samantha smiled. *I should think more than hello when I see him.*

She was gone.

Maddie closed the door.

El Paso, Beau and Samantha gone off to El Paso. Why should I mind? He is what he is. I've known from the start. *"Miss me while I'm gone,"* he says. *Fool girl. Might he miss the fool girl? Not bloody likely.* "I make him *comfortable,"* he says. *What's to be made of Samantha's charms? What sort of comfort comes of that? Why should I mind? He makes me uncomfortable. I do mind. Damn it!*

Santa Fe Trail

Samantha held a handkerchief to her nose. Two days of eating dust in the company of a drummer and a miner both in desperate need of a washtub and a bath found her desperate for solid ground, fresh air, and a bath of her own. To make matters worse the drummer had a fondness for ogling her with undisguised interest. It almost matched his fondness for the flask he carried in the recesses of his coat. Ordinarily she brushed such things aside, but in the confined discomfort of the coach she had few opportunities to deflect his clumsy attempts to engage her. The window being for all intents and purposes her only avenue of escape, her eyes had grown red-rimmed and irritated by the incessant dust clouds.

"Whoa there!"

The stage lurched as the traces slacked and the brake engaged. The driver's call to the team carried an urgency unfamiliar to a routine rest stop. The miner leaned out his window.

"Shit! Road agents." He tried to stuff his poke under the seat.

The drummer grasped his midsection, undoubtedly the location of his money belt.

"Everybody out! Throw down your guns."

Interesting, that sounds like a woman.

The miner tossed out an old cap and ball army that might have done its shooter more harm than any intended target. He followed it out the door. The drummer followed him, hands in the air.

Samantha hesitated, hefted her purse, and opted to play the hand. She went so far as to allow the drummer to help her down, playing the role of her helpless gentle sex. Two masked bandits held the stage, one a rather nondescript man on a bay horse, the other a shapely female with long dark hair and dark eyes to match. She held her gun on the driver.

"See what them passengers has got to offer."

The masked gunman stepped down and wrapped a rein around the right front wheel.

He started with the drummer.

"Hand over the money belt."

"What money belt?"

"You're a drummer. You deal in cash. Now hand over the money belt before I decide to take it off your corpse."

He dropped his hands to his shirt buttons with trembling fingers. He unbuckled the fat purse and slid it around his girth.

"Drop it and step away." He gathered the belt and threw it over his shoulder.

"Now, your poke." He leveled his .44 at the miner.

"Ain't got no poke."

The bandit shook his head. "I'm gonna look in that coach. If I find gold, that lie gets you a case of lead poison." He cocked the gun.

"I'll get it."

The gun muzzle tracked the miner back to the coach.

With both bandits occupied, Samantha saw her chance. She drew her pearl-handled .32 pocket pistol from her purse and shot the man in his gun-hand shoulder, effectively disarming him. The shot caused the masked woman's horse to shy, shaking her gun hand offline. Samantha spun into an instant crouch and fired a second shot at the front hooves of the woman's horse. The horse reared, directing the bandit's return shot harmlessly into the air. The horse bolted, pitching the woman to the ground with a stunning blow. Samantha stood over her, gun cocked, by the time she could gather her senses.

"Drop the gun."

She did. "Who the hell are you?"

"Your worst luck, now on your feet."

The wounded bandit bent to pick up his dropped gun with his good hand. The miner stepped on the gun with one boot and mule kicked the bandit in the head with the other, sending him reeling over backward.

The driver recovered his gun and trained it on the woman.

"Cover her," Samantha said. She drew handcuffs out of her purse and cuffed the woman's hands behind her back. "Now, over there beside your partner. C'mon down, driver, and keep an eye on these two while I get my spare cuffs out of my valise."

The driver scrambled down from the box, gun in hand, still not believing what had just taken place.

Samantha found her valise in the boot and retrieved her cuffs. The wounded man staggered to his feet. She fitted him with the cuffs.

"Easy with them things, I'm shot."

"You might have thought about that before you tried holding up this stage. Now, let's have a look at you." She pulled the bandana down, exposing a sallow-eyed scowl with a rough shave. She turned to the woman. "Now you." She unmasked the woman. "Belle Spice, unless I miss my guess. Wells Fargo will be pleased to hear your road agent days are over. Him too if he rides with you."

"Who the hell are you?" the woman demanded again.

"Samantha Maples, Pinkerton Agent."

"Well I'll be." The driver shook his head.

"Put these two in the coach." She turned to the miner. "You up to ridin' shotgun watch of these two with me?"

He nodded. "Yes, ma'am."

"What about me?" the drummer asked. "With them two inside, there won't be room for me."

Samantha smiled to herself. "Looks like that leaves two choices. Ride one of those horses or up top with the driver." *Either way, I don't have to look at you the rest of the way to Santa Fe.*

CHAPTER TWENTY-SIX

Santa Fe

The stage from Denver rolled into town a couple hours late. The stationmaster sent for the sheriff and a doctor at Samantha's request. She and the old miner waited in the coach with their prisoners until Sheriff Davis Hominy arrived with Deputy Bob Laury.

"Look what we have here, Belle Spice," the sheriff said. "We've been saving a cell for you for too long now. And it seems they've got you trussed up good as a Christmas goose. Attempted robbery, I'd guess." He glanced at the miner. "You responsible for this?"

He tossed a nod at Samantha.

The sheriff registered surprise.

"Samantha Maples, Pinkerton Agency. I trust you can hold these two while we figure out who has the most pressing claim on them."

Hominy recovered his manners and tipped his hat. "Only too happy to oblige, ma'am. Let's get them out of Wiley's coach and up to the jail. Wiley, I'll need a statement from you."

The driver nodded.

The sheriff and his deputy stepped back from the coach. Samantha motioned her prisoners to climb out. She followed the prisoners with a word to the miner.

"Thanks for your help, Everette."

"No trouble a'tall, Miss Maples. I figure we're all mighty grateful we had you along."

The driver nodded. Even the drummer agreed, though he still seemed a bit sour for having to eat dust on the way into Santa Fe.

"Jail's just up the street." The sheriff led the way. Deputy Laury swung in beside Samantha.

"How'd you manage to subdue these two?"

"They didn't pay enough attention to what a woman might do." She lifted her chin at the back of Belle Spice. "You'd think a woman in her line of work might have more sense than that."

"A woman in her line of work ain't sayin' much for sense."

"Shut up, Maples," Belle said over her

shoulder.

"Oh, I'll have my say all right Belle, in court."

The sheriff's office and jail didn't amount to much. A two-room adobe with three cells in back. Deputy Laury locked Belle in one cell and her accomplice, one Hank Toller, in another.

"What do I do about privacy in here?" Belle demanded.

"Use your blanket," Laury said.

"How do I stay warm?"

"Use your blanket." He closed the office door.

"Coffee?" The sheriff poured himself a cup at the corner stove.

"Please." Samantha smiled.

"What do you want me to do with them two?"

"Charge them with attempted stage robbery and hold them. I'm on my way to El Paso on another case. I'll wire Denver before I catch the Butterfield stage. They should figure out what to do with them by the time I get back."

"How long do you figure to be gone?"

"Hard to say. It depends on the case. A couple weeks to a month if I had to guess."

"They'll be waitin' when you come back."

"If anything changes, I'll wire you."

"We'll be here."

Tucson

Hot as Hades and these people put Mexican chilies on everything. Cecile could feel perspiration being sucked out of her skin by the dry air even as she stood on a shaded boardwalk. She squinted through shimmering heat waves across Central Avenue to the gold-lettered sign, Tucson Citizens Bank. Desert heat served only to increase her desire to get this infernal operation over with as fast as possible. She had an unshakeable discomfort that the big handsome detective would be on her trail soon enough. By rights he shouldn't be. Distance and time were on her side this time. They should have been in her favor up north too, but they weren't. The thirteenth bond might explain it, but for some reason she couldn't dismiss, she had a strong feeling he would come onto her sooner than expected. She squared her shoulders and crossed the street.

She stepped up the covered boardwalk to the bank entrance. Inside, the lobby took on a muted glow in contrast to the brilliant white-hot light out on the street. She gave her eyes a moment to adjust as she found the banker at a desk near the vault. She summoned her most disarming charm and crossed the gleaming floor. He looked up and followed her approach.

"Good afternoon. May I help you?"

She smiled. "I hope so. I'm in need of a letter of credit."

"I see. Russell Mason at your service. Please have a seat."

She made a show of arranging her dress properly.

"And what amount are you seeking, Miss . . ."

"Templar, Cecile Templar. One hundred thousand dollars."

He lifted a brow. "That's a rather large sum. Collateral?"

She handed a bond across the desk. He studied it.

"Texas & Pacific, we're quite familiar with the railroad. We do some of their business locally. This shouldn't be a problem."

She flashed him a fetching smile. "Splendid, when might we conclude a transaction?"

"I shall need the approval of the board for a transaction of this size. As it happens we are scheduled to meet day after tomorrow. I should think we could arrange the necessary documents in three days' time."

She tried a small pout. "I was hoping for

something rather sooner than that."

He shrugged. "Bank policy, I'm afraid the matter is out of my hands."

Damn. Now what? Take the bond and leave? We'll never finish this business at this rate. "Then I seem to have no choice but to wait."

"I'll need the bond to prepare the documents. Give me a moment to make out a receipt."

The banker hurried up the street to Sheriff Hardy's office. He found him at his desk.

"Afternoon, Russell. What brings you out in the afternoon heat?"

"This." He drew the bond out of his folio and handed it to the sheriff.

"You suppose this is one of the counterfeits I got the alert on?"

"That's hard for me to say. It's a very good one if it is. If I had to venture a guess, I would say it is. We don't see Texas & Pacific bearer bonds in the amount of one hundred thousand dollars every day, let alone presented by an attractive woman in need of a letter of credit."

"It all fits the pattern Colonel Crook warned us about."

"It does indeed."

"Where's the woman now?"

"I don't really know. Most likely the hotel. I stalled for board approval. She's to come back in three days."

"Good. I'll wire Colonel Crook. I expect he'll want her arrested on suspicion if nothing else."

"I hope we're right. Banks don't prosper having good customers arrested."

Shady Grove

I arrived that Saturday morning with a renewed sense of purpose. I'd posted the manuscript for the first book on to a second publishing house in New York. As the colonel predicted, Penny was full of encouragement over the rejection and soon had me feeling my old self again. That self reminded me of the reason for my determination to succeed, for Penny's affectionate encouragement left me breathless and desperate for somewhat more than a porch swing.

The colonel sat in his chair on the veranda, dozing in the morning sun. I drew up a chair and cleared my throat. He snapped awake.

"Ah, Robert. There you are. I was beginning to doubt you'd come today."

I checked my watch. On time as usual. "Sorry for being late."

"Very well then, just don't make a habit of it."

He glanced over his shoulder. We consummated our weekly whiskey exchange.

"There now, that's settled. Where were we?"

I ruffled the pages of my notebook. "The Tucson sheriff, Hardy, I believe, was the name, reported our bogus bondsman in town."

"Oh yes. I wired him to expect Longstreet and Cane. My telegram caught up with them in El Paso. They caught the next train west."

Chapter Twenty-Seven

Texas & Pacific Westbound

The train highballed through a starlit desert night, haunted by the mournful wail of the whistle. Cane stared into the darkness beyond the coach window. He couldn't sleep. With luck, they were about to catch up with the counterfeiters, at least those who passed the paper on the street. Colonel Crook's big fish challenge gnawed at the back of his mind. If the people passing the paper were in fact low-level operatives, how could they be played to expose those responsible for the scheme? It would be too much to think the people they were about to encounter would willingly reveal the identity of those responsible. Given the sophistication of the operation, it wouldn't be surprising if the foot soldiers didn't even know the identities of those behind it all. What did they have to go on?

Banks got stuck with the paper. They issued letters of credit. Those documents were cashed in favor of Continental Express money orders. Those orders disappeared in anonymity. The field operatives must at least have a hand in that. That was a trail they might follow. How could they expose that part of the operation? He rubbed the bridge of his nose between thumb and forefinger. Each thread he picked at, it seemed, led only to another unanswered question. They couldn't simply apprehend the woman passing the paper. They'd have to follow her to the disposition of a letter and the purchase of a money order, but how?

He listened to the rattle of the rails. The germ of an idea crept into his thoughts. They'd need the bank to cooperate. What banker in his right mind would put that kind of money at risk? A banker who wasn't at risk, that's who. A slow smile tugged at the corners of Cane's mustache. That's it. Perhaps two can play at this game. At last he allowed the rattle of the rails to weigh on his eyes.

Tucson

Early morning light chased the train across the Sonora desert. Ancient saguaro lifted powerful arms in victory over a harsh land as the train rumbled west. Cane mulled his

270

plan against the light of day. *Would it work? It might. Then again, could people this clever be that careless? They were criminals. Of course they could.* Besides he couldn't come up with another way to go fishing without risking the fish they had on the line.

The rattle of the rails slowed. The scattered outskirts of Tucson rolled past the grime-stained window. The train turned northwest, swaying through an ever thickening clutch of adobe, stone, and frame construction, crosshatched along broad dusty avenues. The architectures tossed a mire of Spanish and Victorian design, adapted to desert surroundings by the presence of broad-shaded porches sheltering each floor from the blistering effects of the sun. Round, spired cupolas crowned two- and three-story structures, reminiscent of the widow's walks common to seaside New England. The need to overlook the surrounding sea of sand gave vigilant reminder to past threats of hostile Indian attack.

A whistle blast announced their arrival. The train slow rolled into the station, followed by the steel complaint of brakes and a rush of steam. Cane hauled his valise off the overhead rack and nudged Longstreet awake across the aisle.

"Up and at 'em, prince charming, time to

go to work."

Longstreet rubbed his eyes, stretched, and followed Cane to the car door.

A blast of desert heat, blinding light, and gusty wind greeted Cane as he stepped out on the platform. Central Avenue beckoned west across the street from the depot. Longstreet fell in at his side.

"Where we headed?"

"Crook's telegram said we should look up Sheriff Cole Hardy. He's one of ours. Then we go to the bank and see if we can lay a trap for our paper hanger."

"You got something up your sleeve?"

"I hope so."

"Mind filling me in?"

"Patience is a virtue, Beau. I'm gonna chew that cabbage soon enough, no sense chewing it twice."

A west wind braced the walk up Central Avenue to the heart of the business district. A squat adobe with a weathered sign marked the sheriff's office. Cole Hardy sat at a cluttered desk in a small office that fronted the jail. The weathered officer eyed his visitors with a flint-hued gaze. Cane handled the introductions.

"I expect we should get right over to the bank. Russell Mason, the cashier, has about run out of reasons to stall that woman,"

Hardy said.

He led the way across Central Avenue and up the block to the bank. He introduced Longstreet and Cane to the banker. They pulled up chairs and sat around his desk. Cane came right to the point.

"When is the woman coming back for the letter?"

"I expect she'll be here in the morning."

"That doesn't give us much time."

"Don't take no time a'tall to arrange an arrest," Hardy said.

"We don't plan to arrest her right off. She doesn't work alone. We need her to lead us to her contact. This is a professional operation. I suspect the woman and likely her contact are low-level operatives. The big fish is whoever is behind the scheme."

"But won't she cut and run when she doesn't get her letter?"

"We're going to give her a letter."

That got the banker's attention. "Surely you don't expect me to put the bank at risk for one hundred thousand dollars."

"I didn't say that. I said we are going to give her a letter."

"Sir, a bank letter of credit is a fiduciary instrument."

"That's why you are going to give her a letter of credit acceptance."

"I've never heard of such a thing."

"Neither have I. I just made it up. You're going to give her a letter of credit for one hundred thousand dollars, subject to the bank's acceptance when presented for payment. That last part is in the fine print at the bottom."

"An instrument such as that would be worthless. No one would accept that for cash."

"Exactly. I'm betting the woman doesn't read the fine print and leads us to her contact and maybe the big fish."

"You're asking this bank to participate in what amounts to a fraud. Most irregular."

"So is that bond. Now where is the Western Union office?"

Samantha fought the desert breeze, managing her skirts on the walk up Central Avenue from the depot. She spotted them crossing the street. She might not have noticed the three of them except for the fact Cane and Longstreet made such an unlikely pair. Curious, she passed the hotel and continued on. They'd gone into the sheriff's office. That explained the third man. A little farther up the block she came to Tucson Citizens Bank. That explained where they came from. She almost wouldn't have to follow them. She hurried back to the hotel.

The registration clerk ogled her across the lobby. She smiled to herself. This should be easy.

"Good afternoon, madam. How may I assist you?"

She smiled. "I need a room."

"My pleasure." He spun the register.

She found the entry, glanced at the board behind the counter, and signed. The clerk turned to the board to select a room key.

"Do be a dear and put me in room 203."

He paused, uncertain.

"Silly superstition, I know, but if you'd be so good as to indulge me, I'd be pleased." She favored him with a smile and a flutter of lash.

"Certainly, madam." He slid the key across the counter. "We do aim to please. Do you need any help with your bag?"

"Got it here from the depot, I believe I can manage." She favored him with another smile and started up the stairs to room 203, next door to room 205 and Beau Longstreet.

CHAPTER TWENTY-EIGHT

Next Morning

Waiting tried her patience. Escobar's brooding over the delay didn't help, though he had no answer for it. She was more than ready to shake out the dust of Tucson and move on to El Paso. She strolled down the boardwalk enjoying the warmth of a morning not yet heated to midday inferno. She arrived at the bank moments after opening. The lobby stood quiet as a church at midweek. The banker sat at his desk, studying a ledger over his morning coffee. He watched her approach with one of those insincere half smiles bankers seem able to produce on sighting a customer.

"Good morning, Miss Templar. You're up and about your business bright and early this morning."

"Good morning, Mr. Mason. Is my letter ready?"

"Yes, indeed. Please have a seat." He

opened a folder at his elbow and withdrew the necessary papers. He passed the bond across the desk along with his ink pot and pen. "Endorse the bond here."

She signed.

He replaced the bond with a receipt. "Sign for the letter here."

He slid the letter across the desk.

She checked the amount, folded the document, and placed it in her purse. She rose. "Thank you, Mr. Mason."

"If the bank may be of any further service, please do not hesitate to call on us."

"Good day, sir."

Longstreet and Cane waited and watched from a window table at a café across the street from the bank. Up the block across the street, a heavily veiled Samantha Maples had a similar station in a café where she could keep an eye on Longstreet and Cane. Cecile put the game in play when she entered the bank.

"That's her," Longstreet said.

"You sure?"

He nodded.

"How can you be sure?"

"I recognize the walk."

"I'd almost forgotten your chance encounter."

"Almost encounter." Longstreet smiled.

Minutes later the woman emerged from the bank and turned east toward the seedy side of town.

"Hundred-thousand-dollar robbery don't take no time at all," Longstreet said.

They watched her pass the café across the street.

"Time to go." Cane led the way to the door. They stepped into bright sunlight and paused on the boardwalk letting their quarry put some distance between them.

"Think she's headed for the depot?" Longstreet asked.

"Could be. I'll cross over and follow her from that side of the street. You follow along on this side so we get a good look wherever she goes."

Longstreet nodded. "Nice walk. You'll see."

"I'm sure." Cane crossed the dusty street and fell in behind the woman in the somber gray dress. *Nice walk, leave it to Longstreet to notice such things.*

A block from the depot she turned south toward the red light district. Odd a woman like that headed for that part of town with a hundred-thousand-dollar paper in her purse, Cane thought.

He slowed his pace and looked in a shop

window, keeping his distance so as not to appear to show any interest should she glance his way. She didn't. She continued on down the street with a purpose.

Samantha lost sight of the woman. It didn't matter. She still had Longstreet in view. He quickened his pace, crossing Central Avenue to the southeast corner. He continued south to the next corner. She reached the southwest corner behind them. Cane moved along smartly, his attention drawn down the next block to the east. She rounded the corner and picked up her pace, crossing to the east side of the street as Longstreet disappeared around the corner.

Cecile stopped at the end of the block. She glanced around as if unsure of which way to go. As expected, there was almost no street traffic in this part of town at this hour of the morning. A man entered a cigar store, leaving the street deserted. She turned toward the depot, approaching her destination from the rear. As she approached the street a block south of the depot, she paused again. No customers stirring at this hour either. Good. She turned north to the gated walkway leading up the steps to Scarlet's Red Rose. She shook her head at the ridiculous names given the houses Escobar preferred for his pleasure. She didn't bother to knock.

Inside, morning sun filtered through faded lace curtains turning the shabby parlor a dusty muted gold. The scantily clad trollop on duty eyed her suspiciously over the brim of a steaming cup of coffee.

"What can we do for your Ladyship this morning?"

The sarcasm came with a touch of Irish brogue.

"I'm here to see Señor Escobar."

"He's not to be disturbed."

"He'll be disturbed for me. Tell him Cecile is here."

The girl blinked, started to object, shrugged, and climbed the creaking stairs to an upper floor."

Cecile waited. Moments later the stairs announced the girl's return.

"Come this way."

Cane stood at the corner, looking north to the depot. No sign of her. She didn't simply vanish into thin air. He came back to the rundown three-story Victorian on the corner. A brothel? Hardly likely. Then again, perhaps perfectly so.

Longstreet rounded the corner at the west

end of the block and hurried toward him.

"Where is she?"

He tilted his chin. "In there, unless I miss my guess."

"All right, that sort of establishment is more my style than yours. I'll see if I can find out what she's doin' in there. You cover the back, just in case."

Samantha turned the corner at the west end of the block and ducked back at the sight of Cane. He disappeared into an alley behind a shabby three story at the far end of the block. She checked both sides of the street, but saw no sign of Longstreet. The woman must have gone down the alley or maybe . . .

Cecile followed the young whore down a narrow corridor dimly lit by grimy windows at either end of the hall. Muffled sound seeped under the doors to two of the cribs. The air was warm and damp with sweat-scented musk. The girl reached the end of the hall, rapped on the door to the right, and continued back down the hall to the stairs.

"Come in."

The door opened to a small room, mostly taken up by a bed. A dark-eyed whore sat on the bed mostly covered by a brightly colored shawl. She smoked one of the Mexican's vile cigarillos. He stood at the foot of the bed buttoning his britches.

"Pardon the interruption."

"No trouble where money is involved. The letter, please."

Longstreet stepped into the parlor and looked around, allowing his eyes to adjust to the light. A stair creaked under the step of a young girl clad in a loose-fitting chemise. She smiled her most inviting customer smile. He smiled back.

"Can I help?" Her eyelashes fluttered.

"I'm looking for the woman in a gray gown who just came in."

She pulled a pout. "Don't know what you're talkin' about."

He drew a five dollar gold piece from his pocket. "This help?"

She snatched the coin. "Third floor last room on the right. You didn't hear it from me." She smiled again. "When you're finished, I could still be some help."

Longstreet tipped his hat and started up the stairs. He paused on the third floor landing. The hall was empty. He started down the corridor. By the sound of it two rooms were occupied as one might expect. As he reached the end of the hall he heard voices coming from the room on the right. One of them was clearly that of a man. He drew his pistol from its shoulder rig and listened. Normal conversation didn't carry through the door. They'd be surprised. He threw the door open. The whore screamed.

"Nobody move!" He trained his gun on the man.

The man, Mexican by the look of him, lifted his hands. Alert black eyes flashed around the room.

"Drop the gun."

Longstreet remembered the sound of her voice. "Evanston, wasn't it?" He cut a sidelong glance. "You're much prettier when you're not pointing a gun at a man."

Click. She cocked the gun for emphasis.

Nickel-plated pepper box, .41 caliber lethal at this range. He dropped his gun.

The Mexican snatched it up and stuffed it in the waistband of his trousers.

"Cover him," Cecile said. She stuck her head around the open door. "No one's coming yet, but his partner is likely nearby. What shall we do with him?"

Escobar drew his knife.

The whore stifled a scream. "You ain't gonna cut him up here in my crib!"

"Shut up or you're next." He turned to Longstreet. "You, on the floor, facedown, hands behind your head."

Longstreet turned around and lay face-down, as instructed. He spread his legs in position to take the man down with a scissors kick when the man got close enough. It would probably get him shot but somehow that seemed a better option to having his throat slit.

"Drop your weapons, both of you!"

"Samantha, darlin', you've never looked lovelier, widow's veil and all."

"Save it, Beau. Now, drop those weapons."

Escobar dropped his knife. Cecile let the derringer slip from her fingers. The cocked gun discharged a thunderous blast in the small room. The bullet imbedded harmlessly into the floor. Escobar leaped out the window to the fire escape and raced down the steps two at a time.

"I got her, Beau. After him!"

Longstreet stuck his head out the window. A shot from his own gun greeted him. He ducked back inside.

The gunshot came from somewhere on the upper floors of the house. Cane couldn't place it from his position in the back alley. He drew his gun and started for the street. A second shot exploded followed by the clump of boots. Cane reached the mouth of the alley just as a man reached the ground from the fire escape and disappeared around the corner. Cane ran after him. As he rounded the corner at the front of the building he saw the gunman running up the street toward the depot.

"Stop!"

The dark-skinned man turned and fired.

Cane dropped to one knee and took aim. He fired. The fugitive disappeared behind the station onto the depot platform. A column of black smoke rising into a clear blue sky signaled the man's intentions. Cane ran up the street to the depot.

"All aboard!"

He skidded to a stop at the platform and peeked around the corner. The conductor waved his lantern and stepped off the platform to the caboose. The whistle hooted. The engine belched smoke, brakes released. Couplings clattered as the train began its roll. Cane started across the platform drawing fire from the open door of a freight car. He ducked back behind the depot. The train picked up speed.

Longstreet huffed up beside him. "Where is he?"

Cane lifted his chin at the back of the train. "What about the woman?"

"Samantha's got her."

Cane nodded. "You two get her over to the sheriff's office. I'll wire Crook. Maybe he can arrange to have someone pick up our boy in El Paso. With luck we may be able to pick him up on our way back to Denver."

CHAPTER TWENTY-NINE

Longstreet found Samantha and a sullen Cecile seated on the bed in the whore's crib at Scarlet's Red Rose.

"Did you get him?"

Longstreet shook his head. "He caught the eastbound right on time."

"Damn." She handed him Cecile's derringer. "You keep her covered while I search the place."

"You got a name you prefer to use?" Longstreet said.

No answer.

"It'll go easier on you if you cooperate."

She studied her hands folded in her lap.

Samantha rummaged through a battered leather traveling case. "Look what we have here, one, two, four more bonds. Unless I miscounted that makes twelve."

"Any sign of the plates or the bank letter?"

She shook her head.

"Then they're not out of business yet."
He caught the woman's eyes. "The price of
your cooperation just went up. How about
it?"

Silence.

"You're not helpin' yourself here. Federal
judges don't take kindly to fraud on a scale
as grand as you'll be charged with. A little
cooperation could be well worth your while.
The Union federals got real good at running tough prisons during the war. Their
penitentiaries aren't places a person wants
to spend a lot of time, specially a genteel
lady such as yourself."

"Forget it, Beau. She'll get what she
deserves and rot for it," Samantha said.

"Cecile, Cecile Antoine."

"That's better. Come along, let's get you
over to Sheriff Hardy's accommodations.
We can have us a pleasant little chat there."

Shady Grove

I sensed we'd come to the end of the line.

"Not a terribly satisfying end to the case."

The colonel raised a bushy white brow.
"End?"

"With Escobar escaping I mean."

"Oh, we weren't done with him yet.
Cane's first telegram advised me to alert
our El Paso members and the local Conti-

288

nental Express office to be on the lookout for someone seeking to pass a rather large and fraudulent letter of credit. By the time his second telegram arrived, we knew the man we were looking for to be a pock-marked ferret of a Mexican."

"An exciting morsel of the tale that shall have to wait for next week." My Penny smiled her best Mona Lisa. "Time for supper."

"Speaking of morsels, Robert, you've no idea."

"So you keep saying, but truly it can't be that bad. You don't seem to be wasting away."

"I would, save for the contraband treats you supply me."

I winced. Could he be giving away our little arrangement? I'd never been comfortable with the idea of deceiving Penny.

"Contraband? What contraband, Robert?"

He smiled, letting me twist on her accusation.

"Candy, my dear. Nothing more harmful than a bit of chocolate to sweeten an old man's disposition." He chuckled at my discomfort.

"I should hope not," she said. "Shall I see you at six then, Robert?"

"You shall. See you next week, Colonel."

He patted his lap robe with a conspiratorial wink as she wheeled him away.

Texas & Pacific Eastbound

The train picked up speed. Tucson fell away to the rear. Escobar seated himself on the boxcar floor. The excitement of the encounter with their pursuers, the gunfight and chase, drained away to fatigue. The rattle of the rails turned drowsy. He fought sleep. He had more pressing problems to solve. They would wire ahead. The train would be searched at its next stop. He needed to disappear, but how? If he jumped the train, he would die in the desert or be seriously injured in the fall.

Inspiration when it came, came from the divine. He indulged himself a laugh as he opened a large crate addressed to the First Baptist Church of El Paso. Inside he found an organ. It took what remained of his physical strength to help the organ jump the train.

El Paso

El Paso Town Marshal Pablo Rojas took immediate action on the wire he received from Colonel Crook. He'd had alerts from the Great Western Detective League in the past to be on the lookout for this or that fugitive. Only last year he'd gone on the prowl for the train robber Sam Bass. This one was different. He'd been instructed to search the eastbound train arriving from Tucson for a Mexican known as Escobar and to take him into custody, if found, on suspicion of fraud. He was also advised to set watch on the El Paso Continental Express office for anyone attempting to negotiate a bank letter of credit in the purchase of a large money order. They'd searched the train and found no one.

Escobar kicked his way free of the fragile nail hold he'd pulled together from inside the crate. Despite the late hour a gusty blast of west Texas heat greeted his arrival. He slipped off the depot platform into the shadows and trudged down the street toward town. The road ahead led to Santa Fe. The Don would not be pleased. They'd failed to complete the job. The woman and the last four bonds were now in the hands of the authorities. He'd been lucky to escape, if facing the Don's wrath could be considered luck. They still had the plates. They need only find another printer and a person to pass the paper. It would be wise to have answers for these questions before he faced the Don. Answers and the proceeds of the letter he held in his case. He needed time to think. He smiled. He knew such a place.

The eastbound Texas & Pacific slow-rolled into the station. El Paso spilled south and west from the rail line between Main and St. Louis streets, the architecture a mixture of clapboard and Victorian. Longstreet rode with the Maples woman. Cane had gotten the sullen prisoner. Perhaps the better, it gave him time to think over the run in from Tucson. Cane stared ahead, mulling the little bit she'd told them. She might be holding out on them, but he doubted it. Her story fit his expectations. Either it was the truth or she was a world-class liar.

Her partner was a Mexican she called Escobar. She passed the paper. He cashed the letters. He worked for someone she'd heard him refer to as the Don. She had no knowledge of where the bonds came from. She was paid to pass them. Escobar wasn't the big fish, but he probably knew the next fish in the sea. With luck they might catch him in El Paso.

El Paso
Hot wind whipped stinging sand across the station platform. Longstreet and Samantha

292

escorted the prisoner to the depot. Cane followed along, calculating his next move. They stepped inside out of the wind.

"I need to wire Kingsley," Samantha said.

Longstreet nodded.

"I'll be back in a few minutes." She crossed the station lounge to the Western Union desk.

"You two can take her up to the marshal's office and have her outfitted for suitable accommodations," Cane said. "I'll get rooms at the hotel and pay a visit to the Continental Express office."

"Do you really need to lock me up?" Cecile said. "I'd be no trouble at the hotel."

"Sorry," Longstreet said. "You'd best get used to your new accommodations."

She pulled a sullen pout, as Samantha returned.

"You and Beau can take our guest here up to the marshal's office. I'll get rooms at the hotel and meet you there."

Samantha furrowed her brow.

"C'mon, let's get this one locked up," Beau said.

Samantha fell in beside the prisoner with one eye following Cane out the door and down the street. Her instincts told her something was up.

■ ■ ■ ■

By the time they turned the prisoner over to the custody of a deputy town marshal and returned to the hotel, rooms were waiting along with a telegram from Kingsley.

"Orders from headquarters?" Longstreet asked.

Samantha read. "Kingsley. Wants me to pick up Belle Spice in Santa Fe and deliver her to Denver for trial."

"Belle Spice?"

"Wells Fargo stage robber. She made the mistake of trying to rob the stage I was on coming down here."

"I'll bet she's the one who tried to rob our stage. We managed to run her off."

"Well done, I'm sure. I managed to put a collar on her."

"You're on a hot streak."

She smiled mischievously.

"I'd best buy you a drink to toast your success."

"What about Cane?"

"Oh, he'll be along."

CHAPTER THIRTY

Continental Express Office

"Marshal?"

"Pablo Rojas." The small swarthy marshal standing at the counter extended his hand. The bored express agent glanced at the exchange and went on with his work.

"Briscoe Cane. Colonel Crook sent me."

"I've been expecting you."

"No sign of our counterfeit friend, I take it."

"Not here. Not yet. Though we think he might be in the area."

"Why so?"

"We searched the eastbound train when it arrived from Tucson and found no one matching your description. The following day First Baptist Church reported an organ missing."

"An organ?"

"Sí. The bill of lading clearly showed the instrument was delivered on the eastbound from Tucson. The crate was found on the station platform empty. Organs are not given to walking away on their own, not even Baptist organs. We think your man threw the organ off the train and hid himself in the crate. We have been on watch for him here ever since. No one has attempted to negotiate a bank letter of the sort the dodger describes. He may be hiding somewhere in the area but it is hard to say where."

"Perhaps not so hard."

"You think you know where to find him?"

"I might. Do you have a whorehouse in town?"

Rojas laughed. "Are you joking, amigo? El Paso has many fine whorehouses."

"Our friend favors them."

"Then we have only to search them."

"Not so fast. We want him to cash that letter to see what he does with it."

"Cash? Now it's my turn. Not so fast," the agent at the counter said.

Cane rubbed the stubble on his chin. He could see the man's point. All we really need is for him to lead us to his contact. He smiled with a nod. *It just might work that way too.*

The whore snored, masked in a tangle of raven hair. Escobar smoked, swirling a glass of passable tequila. The time had come. The Don's anger would only grow stronger at further delay. In the morning he would cash the letter and catch the noon stage to Santa Fe. The whore stirred. He stubbed out his cigarillo and tossed off his drink. Another matter pressed.

Morning sun leaked through the curtains. Samantha put finishing touches on her hair. They'd passed a pleasant enough evening with dinner and enough sherry to set the mood. She'd been somewhat surprised when they parted. Longstreet seemed preoccupied. Her instincts told her something might be afoot with the case, but she had her orders. Deliver Belle Spice.

She collected her small bag and left the room. Beau appeared in the hall at the sound of her latch.

"May I escort you to the stage depot?"

"How very gallant."

"You know me, perfectly gallant. Here let me have that." He took her bag.

They descended the sweeping staircase to the lobby and stepped into the day's bright building heat. He offered his arm as they crossed St. Louis to the stage office.

"About last night."

"What about it?"

"I'm afraid I wasn't myself."

"Anything I should be concerned about?"

He paused. "No. I don't think so."

"Good. Then I'll not give it another thought."

She bought a ticket for Santa Fe and joined Beau on the boardwalk to await the stage.

"About our package at the jail."

"Cecile? We'll bring her along. Report your part in her capture to Kingsley. It's a split."

Escobar entered the Continental Express office. He slid the letter across the counter to a bespectacled clerk.

"I need two money orders. One in the amount of eighty thousand and one of twenty thousand."

The clerk made no reaction at the amounts. Odd, they usually did. He read the letter.

"I'll have to present this for acceptance first. That will take a couple of days."

"What? It's a bank letter of credit. It's as good as cash."

He shook his head. "Not really. It says here it is payable on acceptance." He laid the letter on the counter and pointed to the words with a cracked fingernail.

"I've never heard of such a thing."

"Neither have I, but that's what it says."

"There must be some mistake."

"Maybe so, but you'll have to take that up with the bank."

Escobar picked up the letter. *Mistake? No mistake. It's a trap!*

Outside he turned east on Main toward the stage depot.

Cane watched him from a cigar store window across the tracks from the Continental Express office. He stepped outside and followed along.

Escobar turned south and crossed the tracks to San Francisco. He noticed the couple beside the stage up the block. He didn't think anything of it other than the need to hurry as the stage would soon depart. As he drew closer, he recognized the big detective. He ducked into the next available door. A barber sat in his chair reading a newspaper.

"Need a shave?"

Escobar spotted a room at the back. "You got a bath?"

"Sure thing. Four bits."

He tossed the barber a half dollar.

"I'll have the boy fetch hot water."

The barber stepped outside.

Cane broke into a jog when Escobar disappeared in a doorway. He nearly collided with the barber.

"Where is he?"

"Who?"

"The Mexican who just came in here."

"Waitin' for his bath."

Cane pushed past the barber. The shop was empty. The door at the back closed. Cane drew his gun and opened the door to the bath. No one. A single window at the back of the room stood open. He dashed back to the boardwalk.

"Beau!"

Longstreet heard alarm. "Looks like duty calls. See you in Denver."

He ran down the street, leaving the driver to assist Samantha aboard the stage.

Longstreet pounded up the boardwalk to Cane.

"He ducked out the back," Cane said.

"Who?"

"Our Mexican bondsman. You remember."

"Where'd he go?"

Cane shrugged. "You take the livery stable. I got the train station."

He set off for the depot to the clump of Longstreet's boots retreating in the direction of the livery stable. He checked the sky first mindful of Tucson. No smoke sign.

Good. He cut his eyes down side streets and alleys as he made his way to the depot. He climbed the platform and entered the passenger lounge. A few people lounged or dozed on uncomfortable benches. No sign of the Mexican.

Now what? He'd spotted them. He'd have to run. A train was the best choice. Maybe he'd gone for the livery, or maybe he'd steal a horse. Cane didn't like that option. They couldn't cover that one. Movement in a window on the trackside platform caught his eye. He remembered the Western Union office next door. He drew his gun. Passengers stirred, registering alarm as he cracked open the door to the platform. Freight stood in crates waiting to be loaded on the next westbound. He remembered the Baptist organ. Might he try that again? It worked once.

He was about to check the packing crates when the Western Union office door opened on his right. Escobar glanced around. Cane stepped out on the platform and leveled his gun.

"Up with your hands!"

The Mexican's eyes went wide. He lifted his hands with a scowl.

"Now nice and easy. Drop your gun."

He lifted Longstreet's pocket pistol from

his coat with thumb and forefinger and dropped it on the platform.

"Now step away from the gun and lay down. Hands behind your back."

Cane cuffed him and collected Longstreet's gun.

"On your feet."

"You will never keep me, gringo."

"We'll see about that."

"Sí. We shall see."

"Now, before we lock you up, let's see what was so important you needed to send a wire." He marched Escobar into the Western Union office.

The telegrapher puzzled at his visitors. Things with this Mex got stranger by the minute.

"This man send a wire?" Cane said.

The telegrapher nodded.

"Let me see it."

"I can't do that. You the law?"

"Great Western Detective League."

The clerk shrugged. "Don't mean nothin' to me."

"Marshal Rojas good enough?"

"He ain't here."

"Get him."

Ten minutes later the marshal had the message sent to Santa Fe.

El Anillo, *the ring.*

The colonel yawned. He would soon be overtaken by lunch and naptime. Our session for the day was nearing an end.

"What did it mean?"

He looked quizzical.

"El Anillo, the ring."

"As you shall see my young friend we attempted to uncover the answer to that question. It proved a rather ingenious adaptation of the proverbial Gordian knot. Don Victor and his shadow network made a formidable criminal enterprise. One not easily broken."

"And that's why the newspaper accounts of this case are so spare."

The old scoundrel smiled. "You're getting ahead of yourself again, Robert. All I shall say on that point is fortunate for me."

"Fortunate for you, how so?"

"Fortunate I have more stories to tell and thus a continuation of our arrangement." He patted the bulge in his lap robe and smiled.

"Time for lunch and a nap, Colonel."

My lovely Penny never ceased to take my breath away.

"You can set your watch by this girl, boy. If only her punctuality led me to more appetizing or interesting pursuits, but then I suppose you monopolize her in those regards."

"He's incorrigible!" Penney said, stomping a foot in mock indignation. "He refuses to respect that which is none of his affair."

"Affair is it now. Ah ha! See I've been right all along."

She shook her head and wheeled him away with a wink tossed over her shoulder.

CHAPTER THIRTY-ONE

Santa Fe

The Butterfield stage rocked its dust-choked way into Santa Fe. *El Anillo, the Ring.* Cane couldn't get the message out of his mind. The message was sent to Santa Fe, but to who? What did it mean? Someone in the Santa Fe Western Union office must know something.

"Whoa!" The driver hauled lines slowing the coach as they approached Santa Fe Station. The sleepy passengers awoke, Cecile to the uncomfortable realization she'd been sleeping on Longstreet's shoulder. He smiled.

Across the coach Escobar retained his foul humor, refusing to answer the most basic questions. Cane kept him cuffed for his belligerence.

Longstreet stepped down at the station. He offered his hand to Cecile.

Cane hauled Escobar down.

"Heard we had prisoners aboard," the stationmaster said. "Nobody said nothin' about another woman."

"Another woman?" Longstreet said.

"Lady Pinkerton agent's got Belle Spice booked out to Denver tomorrow. You four make it a full coach."

Cane winced at the prospect of another female prisoner joining the trip. He was a bounty hunter. He never signed on to be headmaster to a school for wayward girls. He kept his thoughts to himself. No need to have prickly women for company.

"Sheriff Hominy's office is just up the street," the stationmaster said.

Sheriff Davis Hominy and Samantha greeted them.

"Well, well, gentlemen. It appears hunting improved after I left."

"Sorry you missed all the fun," Longstreet said with a smile.

"You got room for these two, Sheriff?" Cane said.

The sheriff nodded. He reached in a desk drawer, drew out his keys, and turned to Cane. "This way."

"I'm surprised you're still here," Longstreet said.

"Kingsley didn't have all the details worked out for my package. He'll be out of sorts when he hears I missed out on a part in the collar for Cecile's greasy accomplice here."

"Serves his Lordship right."

Even Samantha took a little wry humor in that.

Sheriff Hominy opened the cellblock door. "We'll have to put this one in with Belle. Don't expect that will go over too well."

"They might as well get used to it. Prison accommodations don't offer much by way of privacy."

Cane motioned Cecile and Escobar to follow the sheriff.

"You got company, Belle."

She scowled. "What the hell is this?"

"Your new cellmate."

"This cage ain't big enough for one, never mind two."

Cecile gave Cane a pleading look. He shrugged. The sheriff opened the cell door and locked her in. He locked Escobar in the next cell.

"We'll be leaving in the morning," Cane said.

The sheriff led the way back to the office.

"Belle will be going to Denver with us," Samantha said. "You've got as much as there is on the other one. The client wants Belle to face her Colorado charges. They'll

307

put her away for a spell."

"Fill up my jail one day and clean it out the next. You do take the prize."

"Some folks think so." She smiled at Longstreet. "After eating dust on that stage for two days, I think it's time you bought a girl a drink, Beau Longstreet. Good day, Sheriff."

Cane got to the Western Union office just before closing. The telegrapher glanced at his pocket watch, annoyed that the end of his day might be delayed.

"What can I do for you?"

"Briscoe Cane, Great Western Detective League." He made the introduction sound as official as he could. "We have a prisoner over in the jail who sent a rather unusual wire to this office three days ago."

"What sort of wire?"

"Two words, El Anillo."

The telegrapher shrugged. "Sounds like Spanish. I don't speak the lingo. What's unusual about that?"

"It wasn't addressed to anyone."

"That can happen. Messages sometimes come in incomplete. It don't happen often, but it does."

"What happened to that one?"

"Probably got thrown away. You can't

deliver a wire without an addressee."

"You mean you don't attempt to have a message resent or clarified?"

"Look, mister. It's closing time. I don't remember any message like that, so I have no way of knowing what happened to it."

Cane held the telegrapher's eyes. Something didn't feel right.

"Much obliged."

The salon at the Palace Hotel offered quiet hospitality to a small early evening crowd. Longstreet and Samantha sat at a corner table.

"I don't suppose I properly thanked you for saving me from having my throat cut the other day."

"You'd have done as much for me. Don't give it another thought."

"It's the only throat I got. I'm partial to keepin' it in good working order."

She eyed him with a teasing smile over the rim of her glass; the candlelit sherry gave her features an amber glow. "If you feel you must be grateful, I'm sure we can think of some suitable expression."

"Well I do feel grateful."

"Good. Then I shan't feel bad about taking advantage of you before you fall back to the clutches of that other woman."

"Other woman?"

"Oh, please, Beau. Surely you must know when a woman has her cap set for you."

He shook his head. "Women, you're all unknowable."

"I'm talking about Maddie."

"Maddie? We had supper a time or two."

"A violation of her strict no fraternization policy. She broke her own rule for you."

"You know me, Sam. Rules is made to be broken."

"We all love a bad boy. Now, are you going to show me some gratitude before we spend three sweltering dusty days packed in a swaying sardine tin with two craven women?"

"Three. Only two's been charged."

They both laughed.

Don Victor sat at a massive desk in his lavish book-lined study. He listened to Vincente's report. He shook his head. The client would not be pleased. He was not pleased. A most lucrative enterprise failed. How could this have happened? How did local lawmen react so quickly to their movements? It was almost as though they knew what to look for before it was there to be seen. Impossible. Perhaps, but how else to explain it?

The wire alerted his operatives to the fact Escobar was in trouble. Now they knew he'd been arrested. The woman knew nothing. Escobar would hold his tongue for his blood oath. El Anillo was secure. For this he could be grateful. Still his share in the five uncashed bonds amounted to one hundred thousand dollars. It was a fortune. The client must still be in possession of the plates. He could print more. Would he? If he did, would he entrust the passing to his ring? Who else could do it? Who else could protect his identity so completely?

"What do we do now, Patron?"

"Find out where they take Escobar. From there we can arrange his release."

"Sí, Patron."

There was little else to do for the moment other than the unpleasant prospect of notifying the client. That and await further instructions.

CHAPTER THIRTY-TWO

Denver

The dust didn't taste any better up top than it did riding inside, but Cane figured he had the better of it. He left Longstreet and Samantha to tend the prisoners while he rode with the driver. The man was no conversationalist and mostly occupied with his team. That too suited Cane.

He wasn't happy with where this case had come to a dead end. The bad guys made off with a sizable sum. He took some satisfaction from knowing they hadn't gotten as much as they'd planned, but short of another bond showing up, the investigation was fresh out of leads. Escobar was the only prisoner who knew anything and he was as closed mouthed as a stone. It looked like the big fish would get away because of it. It could have been worse. The Great Western Detective League put a lid on the losses from a gang of very professional criminals.

Crook knew his business. Privately he had a hunch they weren't finished with the mysterious El Anillo.

The driver hauled lines, slowing the coach for the run up Colorado to the station. Cane's butt cramped in protest to the rigors of the long ride. It'd feel damn good to climb down from the box and put some solid ground under his feet, not to mention a good meal and a night's sleep in a real bed.

"Whoa!" The tired team slowed to a stop. The driver set the brake. Cane climbed down stiff-legged from the box. He opened the coach door and gave Samantha a hand down. Cecile followed. Belle refused his assistance. Longstreet lit down behind Escobar.

"Okay, Princess, let's get you off to a new jail."

"Go to hell," Belle said.

"She's a sweetheart all right. You don't know what you missed ridin' up top, Briscoe."

"I got a pretty good idea. Let's lock these ladies and the gent up at the jail. We've got to report to Crook and I suspect his Lordship will want to hear from you."

"Why does it feel like I get the short end of that?" Samantha asked.

Longstreet smiled. "I'd offer to help with Kingsley, but you've saved my life once already this trip."

"Small thanks for that." She prodded Belle up the street to the jail.

Chicago

The Counselor climbed the broad stone steps to the post office entry. He crossed the cavernous lobby to the echoes of his footsteps. The post box had been empty for several days leading him to conclude the operation had come in for some new delay. This day his visit was rewarded with a letter he expected to contain another money order. It did not. The letter contained bad news. Law enforcement had managed to shut down the bond redemption operation, capturing two low-level operatives and the five remaining bonds. His client would not be pleased to hear he'd fallen this far short of his intended proceeds.

He closed the box and moved to a courtesy counter to consider his next move. The plates were sealed in a bank safety deposit box. Finding another printer with the necessary skill and discretion would be no small task. Then there was the matter of securing paper of an appropriate quality. The printer was a risk they would have to eliminate. The police might not make a connection to the previous contract, but more likely the Pinkerton people would. According to the Don, they'd been on the case, but the real damage had been done by an agency he'd never heard of. He sighed. He added his thoughts to the Don's explanation and re-posted them to New York.

Denver

Longstreet walked the shady tree-lined street to the stately Victorian. *Maddie.* Samantha called him out on it. Could it be? Could Samantha possibly be right? If she was, what did he make of it? Damn good question. He didn't know. The Beau Longstreet he knew, or thought he knew, wasn't given to that sort of feeling. He enjoyed women. He courted the willing. Things ran their course and he moved on. He felt comfortable that way. It came back to him unbidden. She made him comfortable. She said he made her uncomfortable. What good could come of that? He'd told her to miss him while he was gone. Why did he do that? Did she? Of course not. Sam was just teasing him for her own amusement.

He swung through the gate and up the walk to the porch. He paused, wondering if he should knock. Hell, he lived here. Sort of. No, he did. He stepped into the familiar foyer, smelling of beeswax and baking bread.

"Who's there?"

"It's Beau."

She appeared in the dining room, wiping her hands on her apron. An errant tendril of auburn hair hung loose from the pile on top of her head. Flour smeared one cheek. She looked lovely.

"Well look what the cat dragged in."

"I suppose I am a bit shabby after three days on the stage from Santa Fe."

She crossed the dining room to the foyer. "Is Samantha home as well?"

"She'll be along directly. I suspect she's making her report to Kingsley."

"And did you two have a successful trip?"

"After a fashion. We captured two of the counterfeiters we were after and the bogus bonds they were passing. The ringleaders escaped."

"Well at least you had the pleasure of keeping company."

"Miss Maples is a colleague and a competitor at that. There was no company keeping involved."

"Of course not, and none of my concern if there were."

"You brought it up."

"My mistake. Welcome home to you. I'm

sure you'll want to freshen up. Supper is at six-thirty."

"Did you miss me?"

"Did I miss you? I've no intention to flatter you, Beau Longstreet. You flatter yourself more than enough for all of us."

"But, did you miss me?"

"You're impossible!"

"Lovable too."

"Ugh!" She reddened, turned on her heel, and stomped back to the kitchen.

He hefted his bag and started up the stairs. *She missed me.*

O'Rourke House Dining Room

They enjoyed a pleasant supper of fried chicken, biscuits, and summer squash while Samantha and Beau regaled the table with stories of their exploits in recent weeks. Maddie rose and began clearing the supper dishes away. Beau added Mrs. Fitzwalter's place setting to his and started for the kitchen.

"Beau, when you're finished there, might I have a word with you?" Samantha said.

He nodded.

"I'll wait in the parlor."

They finished clearing the table. Beau took his place, dish towel in hand.

"I'll manage here. You go along and see

what your colleague has on her mind."

Frosty. "Are you sure?"

"I am."

Samantha waited on the settee in the parlor. "It's such a pleasant evening. Let's go for a walk."

He followed along, nagged by an awkward discomfort. She took his arm down the walk. Last light filtered through the trees, ruffled by a soft breeze. They walked up the block toward town.

"What's on your mind?"

"Kingsley informed me this afternoon. I'm to return to Chicago on assignment."

"I'm sorry. I shall miss you looking after me the next time some varlet takes a notion to cut my throat."

"I shall miss more than that, though it's likely for the best."

"How is that?"

She lifted a brow sidelong in purple evening shadow. "I know what I am, Beau. You might not be so sure. We could have a good time on mutual terms. It's just that our terms aren't mutual yet."

"I don't understand."

"You will. One way or the other. In this business, we'll meet again. Maybe by then you'll know." She paused in the shadow beyond a pool of gaslight. She tipped up on her toes and kissed him. "Now let's get you back to that parlor, before I create more unrest than I already have."

She said good night in the parlor and climbed the stairs. Beau watched her go. Maddie came out of the kitchen through the dining room.

"You wouldn't have a cup of tea back there by any chance?" Beau said.

"Kettle's on the stove with the tea ball in it. Tea's in the tin on the shelf."

"Care to join me?"

"You are exasperating."

"Does that include irresistible?"

"Agh!" She threw up her hands and started back to the kitchen. She added water to the kettle and stirred the fire to light, adding a bit of kindling to heat the pot to a boil.

"Samantha is leaving."

"Where to this time?"

"Not like that, she's moving back to Chicago."

"Oh, how disappointing for you."

"She did save my life."

"There is that to be grateful for."

The kettle whistled. She poured two cups. "Tea, sir." She led the way to the parlor and took a place at the end of the settee. Beau sat beside her and took a sip.

"I suppose it's for the best," Maddie said.

"That may have been mentioned already. Why do you think so?"

"I shan't have to fret over the two of you making a mockery of my fraternization rules. I'm not terribly good at confrontation. It would have been a bother to throw you out."

He caught the fire in her eye. "Ah yes, the rules. Some rules you know are meant to be broken. Would you have supper with me Saturday night?"

"I, I made that mistake once already."

"And lived to tell about it."

"But you've only just returned. It, it would be rather like, picking up where we left off."

"It would, wouldn't it. Would that be so bad?"

She bit her lip.

"You did miss me."

"I did not!" She set down her cup and balled her fists in her lap.

"You did."

"I refused to allow it."

"You failed. I'll tell you something else."

She turned toward him, eyes liquid in lamplight. He touched her cheek. Her lips tilted to his. He kissed her. Soft and sweet until resistance melted into his arms.

"There's a welcome home to give us both discomfort."

CHAPTER THIRTY-THREE

New York

Jay Gould drummed his fingers on the desktop haloed in lamplight. He eyed Don Victor's letter and the Counselor's notes. The bond operation was blown. Fortunately no serious damage had been done, if one were to discount a half-million-dollar shortfall in the proceeds. Gould was never given to such largesse. He cleared a fast half-million. A man could take some comfort in that. Still the operation had failed. He never accepted defeat with grace. The question vexed him. What to do about it?

They still had the plates. Don Victor represented that he could repair his distribution ring. For his share, of course he could. The Counselor reckoned he could find a suitable printer and paper in time. He cautioned, however, that terminating a second printer might alert the Pinkertons. That eventuality was not to be taken lightly, though from these reports the real damage had come at the hands of this Great Western Detective League, whatever the hell that was. What it was mattered little. What mattered was how fast they closed in on the operation after losing the trail. The dead printer with the thirteenth bond got them off on the wrong foot from the very beginning. The Don's adjustment to the pursuit should have given them sufficient time. It didn't.

Gould was a realist. Games played best when they were solidly rigged in favor of the house, his house. This one had seemed so from the start, only to have the tables turned on them. It was time for the house to cut its losses. The Missouri Pacific opportunity wouldn't wait for paper and ink. True he'd be forced to use his backup plan. He always had one. Regrettably in this case that plan was more expensive than the first, but timely nonetheless. The required financing could be arranged here in the east, safely removed from any meddling by the Great Western Detective League. He huffed out the lamp to retire for the night.

Shady Grove
Colonel Crook's story came to a close on a note of regret.

"The big fish did indeed get away," I said. "That's why there is so little detail in the archive reporting on this case."

He nodded. "That of course and the missing plates. One couldn't allow a crisis of confidence in bearer bond financial instruments. The documents were far too useful in the creation of debt instruments, offering the holder secure liquidity. Any loss of confidence would translate to a loss of negotiability and diminished liquidity. Such a circumstance would doubtlessly have increased the interest cost to the borrower necessary to attract investors to a less liquid instrument."

"Are you suggesting that the victims of the crime chose to mask the counterfeit risk?"

"The victims? Heavens, no. The victims in this case were the banks who accepted those bonds. The bond issuers, railroads in this case, wanted the risk swept under the rug. The victims merely went along with it."

"But why would the banks go along? I don't understand."

"Robert, Robert, youthful idealism. The banks went along for two reasons. The banks who experienced the loss were deeply embarrassed at having been taken in. Banks rely on their depositors' and customers' confidence in the safety and soundness of the bank. The victims were fearful their reputations might be sullied by admission of their loss."

"I see that, but what of those who hadn't been taken in. Shouldn't they have insisted the risk be exposed?"

"You might think so, my young friend, except for the fact that the issuers of these bonds, primarily railroads, were substantial consumers of bank services and valuable customers the banks were loath to oppose. The railroads made their feelings on the matter clear to their banks; and between the banks and the railroads, newspapers came to understand that the public interest would not be served by dwelling on the details of the case."

"But what of journalistic ethics?"

"There is that. Perhaps you could put that to right by your book, though you might want to consider your employer's reaction should you make too much of it. As I recall, you found the sketchy roots of this story in their archives. It's possible they were persuaded to bury the story."

"But why would a journalist bury such a story?"

"A journalist might be reluctant as you suggest, but journalists are employed by publishers. Newspaper publishers are compensated by advertising."

"What does that have to do with journalistic ethics in this case?"

"My dear boy, banks and railroads are advertisers."

"So you're saying the story was buried for money."

"Very perceptive of you."

"And the public trust?"

"Regrettable."

Disillusionment washed over principles I'd long held dear on the walk home. Surely this ethical travesty must be an anomaly. Mistakes were made. They couldn't be institutionalized. My editors would defend to the death the right, no duty, to report the truth. Wouldn't they?

I couldn't indulge myself long on these disturbing questions. Penny and I were to attend a new moving picture show that evening, a western, certain to lift my spirits by upholding truth and justice by heroic adventure. I reached my boarding house with time for little more than a change of clothes. The mail stack that I took from the foyer table and carried upstairs to my room contained a thick manila envelope along with the usual assortment of bills. I glanced at the postmark in the dim light of my small room. I tore it open and read.

My disillusionment disappeared in a flood of euphoria. Tonight would be a night to celebrate.

The film offered a perfect metaphor for the possibilities of life ahead. The handsome hero on the dashing stallion saved the day, dispatched the villain, and rode off into the sunset with the beautiful heroine. We savored it along with our favorite sundaes. We walked hand in hand through a pleasant September evening, enjoying the warmth we knew must soon come to an end.

I waited until we were comfortably seated on the porch swing to reveal the good news. I drew the envelope out of my jacket pocket and handed it to her without preamble or ceremony.

"What is this?"

"Open it."

She knit her brow in the dim light. She turned to me, eyes puzzled. "Is this . . . ?"

I nodded. "They've accepted the book."

"Oh, Robert!"

I must confess, I lost account of what transpired for some indeterminate amount of time after that. I can only recall it to be the most joyous celebration I'd experienced in my young life. When we recovered our breath, she smiled that misty-eyed Mona Lisa of hers.

"Does this mean?"

"Yes. I can't yet say when, but we are on our way."

EPILOGUE

Judges Chambers

"Five hundred dollars! That's ridiculous. Is this some kind of joke?"

The lean dark-complexioned man in a gray suit inspected manicured nails with an air of indifference. "As you well know, Your Honor, my client is not given to outbursts of humor. I repeat my request. You will set bond for the prisoner at five hundred dollars."

The judge scowled. "The man stands accused of passing five hundred thousand dollars in counterfeit bonds and you expect me to set bail at five hundred dollars. Five thousand would be a pittance. How do you expect me to explain this to the prosecutor when your man fails to appear in court?"

"That is your problem."

"So you admit the man will take flight."

"I know of no such intent. I only know that if he does, it will be up to you to offer any explanation necessary for your actions. Now, if you please, let us get on with this. I should not like to report your reluctance to my client. As you know, he might very well take offense to that."

"Is that a threat?"

"Your Honor, I am only a simple counselor. I speak only of my client's disappointment."

"Your client's disappointments are well known."

"Good. Then we understand one another."

"Five hundred dollars, so ordered."

Great Western Detective League Offices
"Five hundred dollars and the man walks!" Cane paced the office in white-knuckled frustration. "What the hell is the matter with the judge?"

"He's not generally given to such lapses in judgment," Crook said.

"Well he sure is on this one. Does he not know we didn't recover the plates? The gang could be back in business in no time at all."

"Something doesn't smell right," Longstreet said. "You think it might have anything to do with El Anillo?"

"I'd bet my long-handles on it," Cane said. "About the only thing I got out of the man after we collared him was, 'You will

330

never keep me.' He knew from the start he'd walk. That's why he sent that wire. Without a stage or train to jump he didn't figure the chances of making it out of El Paso were good. He didn't even put up much resistance when I arrested him."

"You think the judge is involved?" Longstreet said.

"What do you think?"

"I figure we're not finished with El Anillo."

ABOUT THE AUTHOR

Paul Colt's critically acclaimed historical fiction crackles with authenticity. His analytical insight, investigative research, and genuine horse sense bring history to life. His characters walk off the pages of history in a style that blends Jeff Shaara's historical dramatizations with Robert B. Parker's gritty dialogue.

Paul's first book with Five Star, *Boots and Saddles: A Call to Glory,* received the Marilyn Brown Novel Award, presented by Utah Valley University. His *Grasshoppers in Summer* received Finalist recognition in the Western Writers of America 2009 Spur Awards.

Paul's work in western literature gives creative expression to a lifelong love of the west. He gets his boots dirty researching a story, whenever possible from the back of a horse. His work as an author follows a successful business career. When not writing, Paul enjoys riding, working with horses, reading, golf, scuba diving, and sport shooting. Paul and his wife, Trish, reside in Lake Geneva, Wisconsin.

Learn more at www.paulcolt.com.

The employees of Thorndike Press hope you have enjoyed this Large Print book. All our Thorndike, Wheeler, and Kennebec Large Print titles are designed for easy reading, and all our books are made to last. Other Thorndike Press Large Print books are available at your library, through selected bookstores, or directly from us.

For information about titles, please call:
  (800) 223-1244

or visit our Web site at:
  http://gale.com/thorndike

To share your comments, please write:
  Publisher
  Thorndike Press
  10 Water St., Suite 310
  Waterville, ME 04901